FATOU

Return to Harlem

Part II of the saga of a West African girl in Harlem

By

Sidi

Sidi

Published by

Harlem Book Center, Inc.
106 West 137th Street, Suite 5D
New York, NY 10030
Tel: +1/646-739-6429

Warning!
This is work of fiction. All the characters, incidents and dialogues are the products of the author's imagination and are not to be construed as real. Any references or similarities to actual events, entities, real people, living or dead, or to real locales are intended to give the novel a sense of reality. Any similarity in other names, characters, entities, places and incidents is purely coincidental.

Cover Design/Graphics: www.mariondesigns.com
Photography: Alexei Production
Editor: Barbara Colasuonno
Model: Rachel from Cameroon

© Copyright 2006
ISBN 0-9763939-3-X

Gift
$14.95
11/11/12
HJ

113881036   JG

ACKNOWLEDGEMENTS

First of all, I'd like to thank Allah for allowing me to complete this project. To my beautiful family, thanks for being patient with me while my mind was concentrating on getting this novel done.

To my people running the book business in the streets, Omar Traore "Rubbish" from 125th Street, Tony Brown, Balde, Ishmael Sangnan, Massamba Amar Jamaica (Queens), Mustapha, Konate Moriba "le Gouru", Yigo Aboubacar, Abdou Boussou, Abo Ndiaye, 23th Street, 6Ave, Cheikhona Ba, 44th Street, Lex. And a special thanks to the two beautiful models, Sidibe Ibrahime "Papito" and Maimouna Ouedraogo "Mai La Princesse".

Special thanks to: J P Morgan Chase Bank-Harlem, Branch 61, Sean Burrows, Sarah, Jacinth Fairweather, Sharyn Peterson, Sharon Font, Sonya Merriel and Bonita Veal.

To my brother-in-law, Fadiga Aboubacar, Sidibe Hadja, Amy, Sidibe Zenab, and Aicha(Ohio) thank for support and believing in me.

Special thank to my friend, Hubert Daleba Gnolou. I know you been always there for me.

To my best friend, Meite Ibrahim Jean. Thank you for holding me down.

To my friends James W. Martin Jr. aka Jalike Ashanti Heru Herukhati, and Norma van Demark aka Ewunike Adesimbo.

Thanks to A & B and Culture Plus for their support and for believing in me.

Thanks to all of the readers who sampled the manuscript and gave me their feedback. There are too many of you to name individually, but you all know who you are, and I'm extremely grateful.

To my special friends from Sweden, Jaqueline Carleson, Lisa Erickson, and Haddy.

To one of my dearest brothers & friend, Sidibe Siaka, his wife, and two sons. I can't thank you enough for what you have done for me.

To my big brother, Ousmane Fofana "Restaurant bon appetit". Thank you for believing in me.

To my friend Marlon. L. 162+Jamaica do your thing.

To my friend from Burundi, Aimable Rulinda.

To Christine Jordan "28 Precinct Harlem". Thank you for keeping our community safe.

To my brother, Inza Sangare "Brikiki", and Kashan Robinson, best-selling author, of Veil of Friendship. Thank you so much for your support.

To my friends in Germany. Thank you so much for your support.

To my brother-in-law, Graig, and his beautiful wife, Corinne. Thank you for encouraging me.

To my man from Paris, Aaron Barrer, "le Congolais blanc". Grand merci. To my best friend, Ahmed Kaba "Bajo" le prince charmant de New York". Keep doing your thing.

To my friend & partner, Raphael aka Pepe, Trazar Variety Book Store, 40 Hoyt Street, Brooklyn, NY. Thank you for your support.

And a special thanks to Kevin E. Young. If it weren't for you the project would not have been completed.

DEDICATION
I dedicate this book to
Sidibe Arravian. E.Wilson "Missy"
Sidibe Mabana Hallary
Sidibe Mamadi, and Keita Maimouna

PROLOGUE

December 13, 2001
New York City

Fatou "La Princesse" Kone was sitting inside her boyfriend David's plush Jamaica, Queens brownstone, crying uncontrollably while trying to hold a conversation with two of New York City's finest.

To the detectives, the house was a mansion. Det. Sergeant Peterson glared at the huge fish tank built into the living room wall, thinking it probably cost more to build than the row home he grew up in.

"There's no sign of forced entry, ma'am," Peterson said, "so your boyfriend must have known the perpetrators."

So your boyfriend must have known the perpetrators...so your boyfriend must have known the perpetrators.

Det. Peterson's words lingered in Fatou's mind hours after he had left the scene. David was completely paranoid, and he certainly would not have let someone into his home that he was beefing with. Besides, with all the warnings and close calls they had had before visiting David's hometown of Kingston, Fatou was sure her man would've

1

had his heat ready if anything looked suspicious.

"This means that one of my lieutenants must have done this shit," Fatou said to herself.

"Did you say something?" Fatou's best friend, Natali, called out from the kitchen.

"No. I was talking to myself."

Natali sighed before placing her cup of coffee on the table and walking into the living room to join Fatou.

"You know it's been a couple weeks," Natali said. "You're barely eating. Your drop-dead figure has done just that—dropped dead. Pretty soon people will be wondering if you're using that shit you're selling."

"Is this your way of making me feel better?"

"It's called tough love, Fatou. How many motherfuckers do you think David killed in his life? I'm sure you know what karma means."

"Fuck karma, and fuck you!"

"Fuck me, Fatou?" Natali asked. "Fuck me? Since when did you start saying fuck you to me? I've been in your corner since day one, remember?"

"Well, be in my corner and stop badgering me."

"I'm not badgering you, girlfriend. I'm just telling you that some risks come with the territory. When you live a cutthroat life, you can expect to have a cutthroat death. I don't know why hustlers get so bent out of shape when one of their homies dies. It's the t-shirts, the soap on cars, the retaliations on everything moving. Rest in peace! Give me a fucking break. Somebody needed to tell the mothers of all the people your man killed that their kids should rest in peace."

"Leave me the fuck alone, Natali!" Fatou shouted.

"I'm not bothering you, girl. I'm just giving you my opinion."

"Well, when I want your opinion, I'll give it to you. Matter of fact, take my keys and get the fuck out. I won't have your ass in my man's house another second talking shit!"

"Look, girl..." Natali started.

"Not another fucking second! Get the fuck out, bitch! Get the fuck out!"

Natali walked out the door and Fatou slammed it behind her before she broke down in tears and crumbled to the floor.

"Why? Why? Why? Why? Why?!" she screamed.

Two hours later Fatou woke up. She had fallen asleep on the carpet just in front of the door.

"Forget about everything I said I was going to do," she said. "Forget about leaving the game. I'm gonna find out which one of our lieutenants killed David if it's the last thing I do.

"If motherfuckers don't know what no justice, no peace means, they're about to find out. David was the only thing that kept me from losing it half the time. But he's gone now, so what does that mean? Whatever the fuck I wanna do, I'm gonna do. And God help the motherfucker who's behind this shit. Ain't a corner on this earth they can run to. Miss Bitch is back, and she's on a fucking rampage. Let me get up and get my shit together. My fucking vacation is over. It's time to send other motherfuckers on vacations—permanent ones."

CHAPTER ONE

The Bronx Zoo

December 18, 2001

Fatou

I hear this thumping. "Boom boom… boom boom… boom boom". I can't figure out where it's coming from. I slightly raise one eyebrow as if my eyesight will help aid my hearing.

"Boom boom… boom boom… boom boom."

"Shut the fuck up!" I yell.

My head is rocked by the vibration of my own voice.

"Boom boom… boom boom… boom boom."

My vision is blurry, and I can't see where the noise is coming from, but I'm able to make out the empty bottle of Henney on the floor near my head. The bottle evokes hazy memories of the night before. It used to be a full fifth. Now it's only a reminder of how everything that brings you pleasure will also eventually bring you pain.

The tightening in my head is a pain I've become much too familiar with.

"Boom boom… boom boom… boom boom."

The thumping now has a name. It's called hangover. I downed another fifth of Henney the night before last night, too, and my head is paying for it.

"Five nights in a row," I whisper to myself, realizing that I have to get my shit together. *I'll never avenge David's death if I can't even tolerate the vibrations from my own voice.*

"Vengeance, yes vengeance," I mouth quietly to myself, remembering that today is the day I start retracing my steps.

As I cough my drunken cough, I hope it doesn't mean I'm about to dry heave again. I haven't eaten in days and the only things I throw up are the fluids I'm sure my body needs.

I feel myself getting sick, but I don't think it's the alcohol. There's a foul scent coming from somewhere, and I can't figure out what the hell it is.

When I cough again it dawns on me that my breath is beyond funky. I've lived without any regard to my hygiene for damn near a week. Not an ounce of water has touched my body. Not an iota of Colgate has grazed my teeth.

I drag myself up and stumble over to the huge mirror on the wall. It's official. I look hideous.

Maybe Natali is right.

When David was living, I was the sexiest thing alive, hands down. Long silky hair, plump juicy ass, nice big titties, no waist, pretty face, and the most mesmerizing gray eyes anyone's ever seen.

Now I look like some piper bitch. My hair looks dry and brittle, the ass that used to force me to wear a size eight even though my waist was more fit for a five now barely holds up a four. My 34 double D's are now just D's and quickly approaching C's. My face is sunken, and my eyes are the saddest I've seen since watching a story on TV about starving little Ethiopian kids with bloated stomachs.

Losing the man I love has had one helluva negative effect on a body. I'm not sure how I'm even able to get up in the morning. Monday, Tuesday, Wednesday, Thursday and Friday seem to be strung together into one long ass day that will never end. When I pass out, I hope I'll wake up in *Ground Hog's Day,* and David will once again be alive. His death would have then just been a sick, psychotic dream. But the reality of the situation is that in a physical sense my baby is dead, and in a metaphysical sense, I've died a thousand deaths. It's like the spirit has been totally sucked out of my body. I'm just a shell of what I used to be.

I lift up my arms to tug at my hair and the hairs in my nose start to burn. I smell like shit, and I know that cleaning up is the first step to feeling better about myself.

I don't even wait to get upstairs. I take off the nasty smelling clothes and drop them in a pile on the floor. They are so disgusting they practically stand up on their own, about to do a rain dance. They beg for water, but they'll never get it. I throw them in the garbage. I wish I could discard all of my emotions just as easily and start over. Rebuilding my life is gonna be very hard without David.

My head continues to pound as I endure MTA's number 4 train, lovingly called the Iron Horse. As it rattles and shakes and squeals from time to time, I realize that in my already fragile state, I am clearly being subjected to more noise than I can handle.

But the number 4 train is the quickest way to take me from what I consider the legacy of Harlem to what the experts deem a mass of urban blight. I'd gone to Harlem to get my car from Natali, but she was out. Of course she wanted to drive my fly shit and not her own bucket. It wouldn't have been so bad if she had left the keys to it, but she didn't so it's the subway, the fucking 4 train. Just another reminder of how the sweetest sugar can become the smelliest shit.

Promise shatters as the landscape changes from the legend of the Harlem Renaissance with its professional portraits of H Rap Brown, Stokely Carmichael, Dr. Martin Luther King Jr., Malcolm X and the like to the reality of the hood. Graffiti-lined buildings feature carefully sprayed omens—*187, real niggas die yung,* and *enta at ya own risk*—overwhelming hints that I've reached my destination, the scariest place in the city, the South Bronx.

As self-assured as I am, I always hate going to the South Bronx. Ordinarily, I have an advantage over most Americans since I can speak a couple African dialects, French and English. Yet, when the Hispanics in the South Bronx start speaking in their native tongue, I always feel handicapped.

Other than that, the Bronx isn't any faster moving a place than the rest of the city. But the people are much grimier. *More Cuban Neckties are given in the South Bronx in a day than in the rest of New York City in a year,* I've always thought.

At just about the same time twelve days ago, I'd traveled the same route, save for the fact that today my journey started in Queens. I took the F train first before transferring to the 4 train at 59th Street.

I was in considerably higher spirits twelve days ago because David was alive and we had spoken about leaving the hustling game behind us. David couldn't get out as fast I could but he had promised me that he wouldn't be too far behind once I announced my retirement to everyone.

I am definitely having misgivings today on the way to meet Donny, my lieutenant in the Bronx. Yet, my suspicions about my own safety prove to be unwarranted. David ended up murdered inside his own home in the big money district of Queens, not me. And since I know I didn't tell anyone where I was going that day, and since only a few people knew that we'd returned from Kingston, Donny is the intelligent first choice in retracing my steps. I need to find out who he's spoken to. I already know he'll run his mouth. I may as well find out what he has to say.

"What's up boss?" Donny says after opening the door to his place. "It's good to see that you're finally back on the streets. We plan on finding whoever did that shit to David and bodying his ass but we wanna take your lead."

"That's why I'm here," I say emotionlessly. "I need to find out who you spoke to that day."

"What do you mean?"

"Have you ever heard of the Ice Man?" I ask.

"Yeah. George Gervin. He played ball back in the day. His handle on the rock was smooth as shit and his jumper was good money. Everybody knows about the Ice Man."

"Not that Ice Man," I say, looking sinister. "I'm talking about another Ice Man. I'm pretty certain this Ice Man wasn't black."

"Why is that?" Donny asks.

"Because he worked for the Gambino Family. He used to have a partner they called Mr. Softee."

"You're talking about those Mafia motherfuckers. Why are you asking me about them?"

"Because Mr. Softee showed the Ice Man all kinds of shit about chemicals—how to torture a motherfucker for hours without killing him. Or how to kill a three hundred pound man in seconds."

"Are you sure you're ready to be out the house? It sounds like you may need a little bit more rest. You're trippin' right now."

"I'm not fucking tripping, Donny," I hiss. "But I am about to start having some fun at your expense if you don't tell me what the fuck I need to know. I ain't watch that documentary on the Ice Man five times for nothing."

I reach in my duffel bag and pull out a stun gun and a needle filled with cyanide.

"Now, we can do it the easy way or this way," I whisper. "Which way are we gonna do this?"

"What's in that fucking needle? Smack? I don't fuck around with that shit," Donny stammers nervously.

"You wish it was just smack," I say creepily. "But if I tell you, I'ma have to kill you. If I were you, I'd realize quickly that I'm the one asking fucking questions around here."

There's a light knock on Donny's door so I nod my head towards it.

"Open it," I say. "Let's see who else has come to the party."

Two Italian men who look like they belong in the cast of the *Sopranos* walk in and stand quietly but with intimidating expressions on their faces. They look at Donny with their arms crossed across their broad chests.

"I don't know if you ever saw *Casino*," I say. "But I was watching it one night. Joe Pesci's in that movie. He plays a mobster named

Nicki Santoro. That little motherfucker is a beast. He kicks people's asses with pool sticks and all kinds of shit. He's the smallest mother-fucker in the whole crew but the most vicious.

"Then I started reading about the Ice Man. He was one of the cold-est hired assassins New York's ever heard of. Now, on the one hand, there's Nicki Santoro, and, on the other hand, there's the Ice Man. Both of them were enforcers for their crew. It got me to thinking that I love my lieutenants. But, since I'm a woman who's full of raging hormones, sooner or later y'all will start disrespecting me. You may even try to do me in like one of y'all did David in."

"Nah, Fatou," Donny stammers.

"Now see, just like that. I was talking and you didn't let me finish. That's rude."

I look over at the two Italians.

"Do you think that was rude?" I ask.

"It was very disrespectful," they answer.

"I apologize," Donny says nervously.

"Again," I say. "I ain't acknowledged you and you're talking. But when I asked you earlier to talk, you ain't have shit to say. Are you confused, Donny?"

There's silence.

"Now you can speak," I hiss.

"I'm confused," he says. "I don't know what would make you think one of us would want to double cross David. He's been our man for years. That nigga put cheddar in our pockets! Who the fuck would do some slimy shit to David?"

"Exactly," I snap. "Who would bite the fucking hand that's feeding them? Do you know who? Do you know fucking who? A hating-ass nigga, that's who. Y'all niggas who were born here don't know shit about loyalty and honor. All you do is plot, scheme and try to figure out how to bring the next man down cuz you ain't got the vision and know-how to come up with some shit on your own. All you know is that house nigga, field nigga, Willie Lynch bullshit that makes all y'all crabs in a fucking barrel. Well, you got two seconds to open your mouth, you crab-ass nigga, or I'm really about to introduce you to my new friends."

For the first time, the two Italians smile.

"Look, I thought we had an agreement," Donny says pleading his case to the Italians. "Y'all leave us alone, and we leave y'all alone."

"Oh, he thinks she means us," one of the Italians says, laughing.

"Let me tell you one thing," I say while walking towards Donny. "Whatever you do, don't try to touch me. This needle will kill either one of us faster than an AK. Now, granted, with David gone, I don't give a shit about dying. But I will take your ass with me."

"I didn't touch David," Donny says pleading his case.

"Who did?"

"Not me."

"Who did?"

"I don't know."

"Who did?"

"I don't fucking know!"

I look into Donny's eyes. They've turned bloodshot red. Sweat is pouring down his face, and his heart is beating so loudly I can't even hear myself think.

"Who did you talk to Donny, after I left?" I ask softly, barely above a whisper. "Think. You had to tell someone that David and I were back from Kingston. Who the fuck was that someone?"

Donny alternates between looking around the room and up at the ceiling. It's obvious he's in deep thought.

His palms become more and more sweaty by the second. He keeps wiping them on his pants. He knows he's running out of time.

Without speaking a word, the two Italians approach Donny and pull plastic pouches from the inside pockets of their suit jackets. The pouches look like miniature tool sets.

When they lift the flaps on the pouches, Donny sees that they contain needles not tools. His eyes grow wider as he wonders if their contents are as deadly as the needle I'm wielding.

"This shit is supposed to make even politicians tell the truth," one of the Italians jokes.

"Good," I say. "Then it should work wonders on a nigga from the South Bronx. Donny meet my friends. One of them has the same shit in his needle as I do. One of them has a truth serum. If you try to stop him from giving it to you so you can tell the truth, one of us is gonna give you a hot shot. Just relax and this shit will be over before you know it. Bottom line, though, is when I leave this house, I'm gonna know who you talked to. Somebody set David up, and they ain't fucking getting away with it."

Donny's takes the shot in the arm and sways like he can't compose himself.

"He's gonna be out of it for a minute," one of the Italians says. "But then you can ask him anything you want, and he won't lie to you. Wait for him to open his eyes fully. You'll be able to tell if he understands you."

"Good," I say. "I'm finally about to get to the bottom of this shit.

I'm finally gonna be steered in the right direction."

After a few minutes, Donny opens his eyes. It's not long before his mouth opens as well and he gives up all the tape.

I leave his house with my two Italian buddies, resigned to get to the bottom of my mystery. Armed with the new information, I'm one step closer to finding out everything that I need to know.

CHAPTER TWO

The Family

December 18, 2001

After hearing Donny spill his guts, I'm glad I asked my two Italian buddies to leave the room.

"I can't believe that David didn't tell me this," I say out loud while shifting my weight from one foot to the other. "I'm gonna have to handle things much differently than I planned to."

I head back to the check cashing place, hoping to slip into my office without Natali noticing.

My check cashing place is a front for an escort service that my best friend and now partner, Natali, talked me into setting up while she was locked up in an INS center after getting busted for having an escort service. With all of her political connections, she thought that it didn't make sense to let her clout go to waste. Plus, rich mother-fuckers are kinda loose with their money. It made sense to me so I found a nice spot in Harlem and bought it with one of Natali's work-ers, Chyna.

Chyna was gung ho on the escort service, but I didn't want to get busted like Natali so I came up with the idea of using a check cashing place as a front. Customers come in the front door to cash their checks and walk out unaware that the escort service entrance is off to the side around the corner.

Chyna used to run the escort service, but she got her ass blasted. Turns out that she was pocketing the money she told me she had sent to Natali. I questioned her one day about it, and she started hemming and hawing but not saying shit. I chipped her up a little bit, and the bitch had the nerve to tell David she was gonna squeal on him. He bodied her ass without hesitation. David wasn't one to let shit ride. He always said, "Handle your business or your business will find a way to handle you."

I realize that was one of the reasons why David always wielded so much influence over everyone.

"He always negotiated from a position of power," I whisper to myself. "What better way is there to reclaim our organization's position of power than to lock down the streets? Once I handle the street credibility issue, everything else will fall into place."

I got it, I think after finally coming up with a master plan.

"Politics is a bitch," I sigh out loud before leaving my office and head to the escort service.

Natali is stunned to see me walk in. "I didn't think I'd see you around here for a long time after our last conversation."

I ignore the comment and guide the conversation exactly where I want it to go.

"How hard do you think it will be for you to get back in good standing with your connections at City Hall?"

"I've always kept close ties with them, even when I was locked up.

15

But I thought you didn't want me involving them again in anything we're doing over here."

"Yeah, yeah, yeah," I say. "But we have to get our shit tight again. Any advantage we have needs to be explored and used to the fullest."

"Well, I can talk to them. What do you want me to say?"

"Nothing yet. Just do what you gotta do to get back in their good graces. That'll give me some time to get everything together in my head."

"Alright, I can do that," Natali says. "I'll start making some phone calls right away."

"That's what's up." I turn, walk out the door, and head back to my office. "This shit is gonna be like taking candy from a baby."

"Can I speak to Big Tony?" I ask the girl who answers the phone for the Cicero crime family. "It's the African princess."

Tony Cicero eagerly picks up the phone when he learns I'm on the line.

"It's a beautiful day now," Tony chuckles in his heavy Italian accent. "The gods must be smiling down on me."

"You're so charming, Tony. No wonder you have to beat the girls off with a stick."

"Well, you wouldn't have to do that, princess. Whenever you're ready for me, you let me know."

"You're too much, Tony," I flirt. "I'm sorry I called you unexpectedly like this but I can use your help."

"Forget about it. You know I'm always here for you. And my condolences. David was a good man, a really good man."

"Yeah. That's what I want to talk to you about. Now that he's gone,

I'm not sure people will respect me the same way. Pretty soon they'll be coming at me left and right with foolishness."

"Say no more. When can you meet me for lunch or dinner so we can talk about it?"

"Whenever. You're doing me a favor. Just say where and when and I'll be there."

Tony wants to meet at Anastacio's, a pomp Italian restaurant in Little Italy, on Hester just below Mulberry. It has a vibrant atmosphere, flaunting nostalgic Italian red-checkered tablecloths and family portraits. The main dining room is stunning with intimate table settings for two and accommodations for groups up to fourteen. Such is why Anastacio's is routinely the choice for New York's connected Italian underworld—you never know when the whole family is gonna show up.

I tell myself that I'm definitely gonna have to change my clothes and knock Tony off his feet when I walk in to Anastacio's.

Natali is even thinner than I now am so I borrow one of the dresses I bought for her. Her mind is always on the escort thing which makes her style somewhat hoochie. Me, on the other hand, I love to be sexy but never hoochie. To me, hoochie is raunchy, and you can't be classy if you look raunchy.

The size 4 Baby Phat dress clings to me like it was painted on. I love the light blue accent beads sewn onto the royal blue fabric so I decide to accessorize with a light blue leather jacket and matching leather pumps. The three-inch heels do wonders for my shape; they make my ass seem like the apple bottom is back. Even my thighs look luscious again. I guess there is some hope for getting my body back.

17

Yet, even without it, I look damn good right now. Tony will be Silly Putty in my hands.

When I arrive at Anastacio's, the aromas pull me like a magnet. I remember how hungry I am. I haven't eaten in nearly a week. As I walk in the door, I promise myself to not make a pig out of myself.

I see that Tony is trying his damnedest to play it cool and act like he's unphased by my presence. But I know his act is a bunch of bullshit.

In his dark Italian suit and tie and imported Italian designer shoes, Tony peruses the menu as he lectures me on how everything at Anastacio's is homemade with the freshest ingredients. His plump cheeks and taut jawbone seem unusually jovial for a no-nonsense crime boss. I know I'm getting to him. I just have to keep playing things cool.

I don't protest when Tony tells the waitress to pour us two glasses of imported red wine. But I do let him know that I have to eat something before I start drinking.

"With my grief and all, Tony, I haven't eaten in days. I don't want to get sick and ruin our lovely dinner."

He understands and doesn't make a big deal of it. I think I even scored a couple points when I hinted about being an emotional wreck. Men always want to feel like they can aid a damsel in distress—especially macho Italians like Tony.

Tony orders himself veal Parmigiana with a Caesar's salad and some type of spinach soup.

He tells me that he's watching his carbs and doesn't want overdo it.

"You on the other hand," he says, "We have to put the meat back

18

on your bones."

He orders me a sixteen-ounce London broil, a baked potato with sour cream and chives, and the biggest lobster I've ever seen in my life. There's no way I'm gonna be able to eat all of it.

Tony perks up even more when Frank Sinatra starts crooning *I Did It My Way*. As he starts singing along with the song, he looks kind of cute. His big cheeks are red, and his body is full of life, totally animated. I realize that's what it looks like when a powerful man let's himself loose. I'm sure that his animated alter ego has my name written all over it. This is the closest Tony has ever been to a fierce black babe like myself. And, to add fuel to the fire, in his mind I have just as much power on the streets as he does. He's probably coming in his fucking pants.

"So, Tony," I say. "Let's get down to business. Let me explain why I'm here."

For forty minutes I reel Tony in. I remind him of the wealth and power that David left me before he was killed. I reveal to him that I'm obsessed with finding and torturing my lover's murderer.

Such violent talk has to be a turn-on for the likes of Tony, but I don't stop with that. I meticulously dip a lobster claw in the drawn butter and suck out the meat. When I notice him staring too hard, I figure I'd better stop before I give the guy a damned heart attack. It's official. He's wrapped around my tiny fingers.

"So let me get this straight," Tony says. "You want my family to help protect you."

"Not exactly," I say. "I want to hire some of the hit men your family controls to do some work for me. I want people you know so that they don't get too high and mighty with their egos. They don't have to be your people. Actually, I'd really prefer it if they weren't your people. I don't want you all caught up in what I have to do. But of course I'll reward you for your help. This city is about to be turned upside down for what was done to David, and I know you already have enough heat. Still, I can't risk using inexperienced hit men who'll mess everything up for me. I need professionals. I'm sure you know a few. You'll get a finder's fee just for making the connection. In the end, your hands will be clean, and no one will be looking your way when the shit hits the fan."

"Such a violent streak in such a pretty lady! How can it get any better than this?"

"You always know what to say, Tony," I flatter.

"Well, Fatou, you're my inspiration."

On cue, I take an envelope out of my Baby Phat purse, hoping to entice him even more. The big bosses love envelopes. I know that Tony is no different.

"I have to go, Tony. Let me know if you can help me."

"Stay for a while," he pleads. "Let's have some fun."

I decide to tease him one last time and lean over and whisper softly in his ear, my breath tickling his insides.

"Business first, Tony," I say. "Then we can have some fun. I promise."

I softly kiss both of his cheeks and switch away happy to be wearing the smallest thong I could find. My jiggling ass in his face is the last image I leave him with. I'm certain I've guaranteed his help.

CHAPTER THREE

Bah Humbug

December 23, 2001

It's not quite a week after my meeting with Tony, and I'm up to my ass with shit to do. It's the day before Christmas Eve, and the orders are coming in like ants scrounging for scraps after a picnic. I don't know if everyone wants to celebrate the holidays or if they want to take their minds off the holidays. Whatever the case may be, my lieutenants keep piling product upon product on my list of raw drugs needed to be stepped on. That's why I'm in the middle of an abandoned house in Brooklyn, fidgeting with one of my two electric generators. I have about two hours worth of power left before I'll have to leave and recharge them, so I'm hoping it's enough time to finish what I have to do.

My electric stove has a pot on each burner. In one is the pure cocaine I'm turning into crack, and the other has a combination of opium, dextrose, powdered milk, Epsom salt and quinine—everything I need to turn fifty kilos of opium into five kilos of high grade heroin. Since Ricco, my lieutenant in Manhattan and parts of Harlem, needs so much of it, I plan to step on the heroin about five more times after this batch is done so I end up with ten kilos instead of five.

For the $500 I spent on the opium and the $500 I spent for the other ingredients, not taking into account what I had to give Natali, I'll see about a two thousand percent profit. I sell the heroin to Ricco for twenty grand a kilo.

About Natali...Quinine is an important ingredient for turning opium into heroin, but you need a license to buy or sell it. Natali knows a doctor who gets shitloads of the stuff but gives it to her only if she blows him first. You'd think she'd do it without complaining since she has been having sex for money for years. But she can't stand the doctor. I have to pay her out my ass every time I need quinine. I'm glad she has oral skills though. Even with the dough I give her, I'm still saving a whole lotta cheddar.

I sell kilos to Ricco at a discount because he moves so much of it in Manhattan. But everyone else buys quarter kilo packs for $7500. Still, they get about twenty-five thousand 100 milligram bags for their soldiers to sell on the street for ten bucks a bag. After kicking fifty grand back to me just because I can get the product and they can't, they walk away with close to two hundred grand after paying their soldiers. That's a pretty penny for kicking out $7500.

The way I see it, everybody is happy. And as long as they're making cheddar, we're all gonna stay happy.

Once I finish cooking the crack, I clean out the huge pot so I can double-up on the stove to finish the heroin faster. When I am satisfied that my witch's brew is fine, I turn to my kilos of pure cocaine.

To my connection, I normally pay eight grand for a kilo of pure cocaine. I step on the pure cocaine three or four times and sell each kilo of processed coke for fifteen grand each. Even without my kick-back, I make over fifty grand per kilo of pure cocaine that I buy. But, with my lieutenants stepping on the kilos, I sell them twice by breaking down the kilos into quarter kilos that sell for about ten grand each. I make another $7500 in profit off the top which amounts to ten percent of the seventy-five grand they stand to make after recovering their initial investment.

Mo' money, mo' money, mo' money.

I forgot that quinine isn't the only thing I get from Natali's doctor friend. He also gives us embalming fluid when we need it, which is all the time since so many people have been fucking with wet lately. In case you don't know, wet is weed mixed with embalming fluid and sold in a small plastic tube with a lid.

With the exception of turning some of the weed I buy into wet, I never step on weed. Real weed smokers can tell if something ain't right with their shit so you never want to end up with a whole lot of weed you can't get rid of. I am satisfied with doubling my money. I buy it for $250 a pound and sell it for $550 a pound. People buy so much weed it seems like I am making more than that off of my money.

With barely five minutes of electricity to spare, I finish packing up the pure cocaine, crack cocaine, heroin, weed and wet and head for the door. I almost forget to wake up Gino Carlotti, one of the guys Tony recommended to me.

"Are you gonna do all this shit in front of me?" he asks.

"Why not?" I ask. "Tony sent you so I already know that you understand that you'd be dead quicker than any fucked up thoughts popping into your head. I just need to hurry up getting my shit together for the holiday business before we can talk."

Gino acts like he doesn't want any part of what I'm doing. He just plops down in one of the chairs I'd brought into the abandoned building long ago, and before I know it, he's sound asleep.

He sleeps like a baby. He doesn't even hear me when I start crying my eyes out again.

Stepping on the pure cocaine and seeing all of it takes me back to the days when David used to rub cocaine on the tip of his dick. I swear he stayed hard forever. I shudder thinking about how much I miss having him inside of me. Christmas just ain't Christmas without the one you love.

"So let me get this straight," Gino says. "You want me to walk up on a set in broad daylight and just start blasting? And you want me to do it in Harlem?"

"Not a set," I say. "A bunch of sets. I want everyone to know that the African girl is back."

My plan is to shake shit up on the streets. And what better time to do it than around the holidays?

We still own most of the street corners but there are several in Harlem that fell off after we had to kill Ken, our former lieutenant in downtown Queens who had also been helping out a little in Harlem.

David and I found out that Ken was selling us out to our arch rival, Salu, who used to own Motherland Taxi—a drug organization that uses taxicabs as fronts and distribution centers. We ended up killing Salu, most of the top people in his clique, and Ken. Now, Motherland is operated without direction by some herb-ass dude named Billy. Billy's also the one holding down the corners Ken used to control.

My crew of assassins are about to fix that shit, but it's not as easy to get away with killing a white person as it is a black. So, when my assassins start dropping bodies, they won't be suspected for a long. Nobody's gonna put two and two together and find out that I'm really the one holding shit down. What cop is gonna be asking questions about me when white motherfuckers are the ones bodying people? And if they do start asking questions, Natali's sucking the right dicks in City Hall again so I should be OK. It's always an advantage to have a sexual beast on your squad.

There isn't much daylight left when Gino and I abandon the abandoned building and jump on the Brooklyn Queens Expressway to Harlem. Still, I want everything to go down tonight, or at least start going down tonight.

As we drive around Harlem, I point out sets to Gino so he can blast them once he and I split up. I'd loved to be with him when all hell breaks loose but I have too much to do right now.

My runner is going to make the exchanges with my lieutenants so I'm following her ass around. She'll be picking up between three and five hundred grand tonight so I'm sticking to her like white on rice. I don't care how scared she acts. I'm not gonna give her the chance to cross me and disappear with gobs of my cheddar. Not now, not ever.

I don't know why I'm so tight with money considering how much I have. Before David died, I transferred all of the money we used to keep in the tunnels into his safe-house in Queens. Now there's money floor to the ceiling in the attic there, probably over 400 million dollars.

Most of that was David's money. Now it's mine. I thought I was living large with the two million I'd made since I started fucking with David. Now, I'm sitting on a gold mine, but I can't enjoy it. I'm too fucking stressed out about living without my baby. I'd give all the money away if I could just bring him back to me.

I don't want to start crying again so let me change the subject. I mentioned the tunnels and the attic in the safe-house, but I didn't say anything about how significant they are.

David had a connection in City Hall that we called Underground. Reason was, he spent so much time in the tunnels owned and operated by the Office of Emergency Management (OEM). Underground worked for the OEM and was always going to these big cabinet meetings in downtown. He always knew what was going on before anyone else.

Anyway, David paid Underground a lot of money so that he and I would have unlimited access to the tunnels. In fact, I still have the keys. But I haven't been in them since 9/11. Before 9/11, there was hardly anyone down there. But once those planes took out the towers, it seemed like a family reunion down there. I guess the tunnels are used for planning sessions in the event of an emergency. And 9/11 was definitely an emergency.

In the chaos and aftermath of 9/11, David thought it was a good time to attack Salu and his squad. We launched an all-out assault on Motherland Taxi all throughout the city.

There was a small problem, however, and that was that despite law enforcement having their suspicions about Motherland Taxi, it still paid it's taxes. It was a business that employed a lot of immigrants. As it turned out, someone from City Hall believed that vigilante citizens had committed hate crimes against Motherland Taxi drivers, most of whom were Muslim.

With Underground knowing what he knew, and as much as we hated to doing it, we had no choice but to take him out.

Now, about the attics in the safe houses. The ceilings in both of David's houses in Queens and the safe house not far from there are extremely high. No one suspects that there are even attics on them. In order to get to them, it is necessary to take elevators through secret compartments in the kitchens.

The unique thing about the elevators is you have to remove paneling from the wall to get to them. And, once you're on them, the paneling replaces itself so no one can see the elevators. If you could get on the elevator fast enough, no one would ever know where you went.

Inside the attics, security cameras monitor the houses, both inside and out. The attics are covered with wall-to-wall steel and crowded with computer equipment. The monitors also display the interior and exterior of every OEM tunnel in the city. So, in addition to being filled with floor to ceiling stacks of money, the attics are my window onto New York City's underground. I know everything about everything. And I know that, soon, I'll be able to resume using the tunnels again.

My runner shows up at her first stop in Harlem and pulls me out of my thoughts. She's about to meet with Ricco.

Ricco is a mix breed—half Italian, half black. His features remind me of The Rock from the WWF, except he's a little taller and wears a ponytail like movie star Steven Segal. Word on the street has always been that he's the illegitimate son of one of New York's true wise guy's, Tony "the Butcher" Mizzonelli. But after what Donny told me when I drugged him, I know that's not true. The Butcher's not his father, but his old man is a wise guy.

I slide down into my seat as my runner and Ricco are about to make the exchange. Like clockwork, I hear gun blasts from down the street.

"Gino must be on point," I say to myself while watching Ricco duck behind the door. I watch my runner take off down the street in my rearview window. Eventually, she disappears.

"Good," I say. "She got away."

As I turn back to Ricco, I see that some of Gino's henchmen have ambushed him. They don't harm him. Instead, they relieve him of the drugs my runner has just given him. I smile. I follow my runner to Penn Station before I meet Big Tony Cicero again.

Tony and I are eating at an Italian restaurant in Little Italy when Ricco chirps me on my Nextel. I give him the number of the pay phone at the back of the restaurant and wait for him to call me back, also from a pay phone. I excuse myself when I hear the phone ring.

Ricco tells me that he's just been hijacked for drugs he just paid for. I ask him how he, a lieutenant, could allow someone to take his drugs, and my runner turned in the money to me. I tell him that he should ask for a Christmas break on the amount of money he has to kick back to me and not try to play me into letting him off the hook for all of it. He tries to explain that he's not trying to play me, but I say, "I'm not beat," and hang up the phone.

I'm visibly upset when I rejoin Tony. Of course he asks me what's wrong so I tell him.

"The shit's starting already, Tony. Ricco's trying to tell me that he just got robbed for the package my runner just dropped off. Problem is, she already gave me all the money from the package. Why would they rob him and let her go? The shit sounds suspect. He's gonna make millions off that package, but he's trying to stiff me for a punk-ass three hundred grand."

"Let me talk to him," Tony says. "I can't believe this shit is happening right now. It's Christmas! But don't you worry your pretty little head about it. Let me handle it. Forget about it. You hear me, Fatou? Forget about the whole shit. It's as good as resolved."

I shake my head and bite my tongue to stop myself from laughing. I know Tony is gonna make Ricco pay me anyway. Plus, the whole situation is gonna make Tony start wondering what's up with Ricco in the first place.

Everything is working out the way I want it to. It won't be long now. The city's gonna regret David's death.

CHAPTER FOUR

Christmas day 2001

I decide to take Natali to David's yacht so we can spend Christmas morning together. I'm still upset about all the shit she said about David, and lord knows I feel some typa way about having her up in his shit, but she's my girl. I would never have survived my ordeal with Lama, Fifi and Patra if it wasn't for Natali.

Lama is the man who paid my parents a dowry, La Dotte, to bring me to America from my homeland in West Africa. I was twelve at the time. He was forty-five.

I thought I was coming to America to continue my studies. But the real reason I was brought here was so that Lama could do whatever he wanted with me. He was a pedophile, and I won't tell you everything he did to me.

But the one positive thing he did do for me was to force me to work in a hair salon owned by one of his relatives, Sister Fifi. She's a money-hungry evil little bitch who paid me sixty dollars a week to work nearly sixty hours a week.

Fifi forced her stylists to have sex with men for money in the back room then kept most of it. Her constant threats to call immigration on us was motivation enough to do whatever she asked us to do. Being a whore is bad enough, but if you have to sleep with a man for forty dollars, it's insulting to know that your pimp is only gonna give you eight. Because I was married to Lama, I never had to have sex with the sleazy men she brought in.

The power she had with the other girls, though, illegal immigrants all, was the constant threat of deportation. Lama was a naturalized US citizen. I didn't have to do what she wanted me to do. The other girls were scared to death of her. That's why I thought a stylist named Patra had sex with everyone. Turns out that that was her reason for having sex with Fifi's patrons, but it why she slept with Lama.

Patra had strong feelings for Lama and thought he would marry her and help her become a naturalized citizen like he'd become after winning the INS lottery and receiving his green card. But, instead, he paid for me to come from West Africa and immediately made me partake in our country's traditional wedding ceremony. To the US, our marriage wasn't legal. But to everyone else, it was. And as much as Patra pretended to be my friend, my traditional marriage to Lama was more than enough to make her hate me.

When I became pregnant, she talked me into letting her perform an abortion on me. I was so young, and I wasn't ready to have a baby. But I didn't know anything about shit like that. I was only thirteen at the time. Anyway, she destroyed my insides, and I almost bled to death. The doctors said that I'd never have children.

Not long after that, Patra started having Lama's babies. So I guess her screwing me up as far as having kids was her way of drawing a line in the sand with Lama. And the funny thing was, that was around the same time I actually started having feelings for Lama. His disrespect for me with Patra made me want him to spite her. But Natali wasn't having any part of that. She constantly told me the best way to spite both of them, and Fifi, was to get the hell away from them and that salon.

I met Natali at Fifi's and she before she became my best customer and best friend. She taught me English, gave me gifts, and showed me how to stand up for myself. She put Vaseline on my face and neck to protect my flawless skin the time I had to whip Patra's cousin Nefara's little ass. She was the only person who frequented Fifi's salon who gave a damn about me.

So, even though I'm mad that she disrespected my man's memory, she's still the best friend I have.

Sitting below in the stateroom in our bikinis, sipping Cristal straight from the bottle is the perfect way to ring in Christmas. The tanning lamps David bought for me creates the illusion that we're not in cold New York City. My eyes are closed, and I'm imagining that David and I are still in Kingston, basking in the sun.

I haven't told Natali yet, but there is a chance that I may be pregnant.

Before David died, he told that he wanted me to have his baby. I reminded him about Patra and the mutilating abortion but he took me to see a specialist anyway. The specialist did a medical procedure on me and told me that I had a fifty-fifty chance of giving birth if I become pregnant. I pray every night that since David is no longer here to love me maybe God will spare my being alone by allowing me to have David's baby. That hope is one of the two things that keep me going some days.

The other thing is knowing that I will make whoever killed David pay royally. That's why I'm meeting with my lieutenants later tonight. I'm going to make the snake that killed David slither his way out of hiding. That's my word. I'm gonna get his ass if it's the last thing I do on this earth.

After Natali and I finish tanning in the stateroom, we dress before my hired assassins arrive. I wanna have some muscle in case one of my team feels the need to act up.

I know they're gonna bitch. It's Christmas day and business is gonna boom when it gets dark. It's funny how feens try to act like they have a little respect by not getting high early on Christmas. If you get high, then just go ahead and get high. Don't try to front like you have some self control over your shit. If that were the case, you wouldn't be selling everything you have for a quick hit.

But I can't be too hard on the feens. They've made me rich, and they're keeping me rich.

While I'm thinking about all of my money, Natali comes to the barroom with a Baby Phat cat suit on. Her shape is all that so the bitch is wearing the shit outta her outfit. Her shape sorta reminds me of Lisa Raye—long legs, kinda tall with a nice butt and nice tits. No, her shit ain't as voluptuous as mine, but she still gets a lot of props for her figure. I hope Natali doesn't plan on hanging around when I'm meeting with my lieutenants. It'll be hard to keep their attention with her looking all sexy.

I decide to wear some militant shit. I have on tight black khaki pants and a camouflage drawstring top. I'm sporting high-heeled camouflage Timbs on my feet and a black scarf on my head. I definitely look like a gangsta bitch right about now.

Natali sees me looking at her sideways so I tell her how I feel about her distracting my lieutenants while I'm trying to conduct business.

"Bitch, you're the one who looks sexy as hell," she says. "You better worry about them lusting over your ass, not mine!"

I laugh at her. She might be right. It's been a long time since I've looked so hot.

My Italian buddies pat my lieutenants down as they come in and collect their heat. They had to know that shit was coming since I used to complain to David about letting them in the crib with their strap on.

Sarge and Rottweiler show up first like they always do. They're holding shit down for me in North Jersey. Sarge used to only handle Newark and alternate with Rott holding down Jersey City. But he lets Rott take care of Jersey City full-time since he's doing so well running shit in Paterson, Plainfield and Rahway.

Aside from Jersey City, Rott controls Elizabeth, Secaucus, Montclair and Long Branch. Between the two of them, they're pulling in close to two hundred grand a week selling some of everything, crack and powder cocaine, heroine, purple haze, wet and Zanex.

As always, they wear their wild, Don King afros and diamond laced patches they call their third eyes. Tonight, they left their six foot snakes home. Normally, the suckers are wrapped around their necks. They knew I wouldn't have any of that shit. The snakes are probably slithering around their million dollar home in Teaneck along with Rott's six namesake Rottweilers.

Natali hands the twins bottled water because she couldn't talk them into having a drink for the holidays

Redd struts in with his sexy-ass self.

Redd, who handles Jamaica, has a face and wavy hair that reminds me of the LA Lakers' Rick Fox. But his body is a diesel the way Mike Tyson's used to be when he was knocking motherfuckers out in the first round. With all he's got going on, he's a terror with the ladies. But that doesn't stop him from moving seventy grand worth of powdered cocaine a week. If you add in his sales of crack and weed, most of the time Redd clears a hundred grand.

Redd starts pushing up on Natali as soon as he sees her. Or is it the other way around? I can't tell. Whatever the case, I hope she understands that Redd's not the type of nigga who tolerates any of his women getting other dick. He has a bunch of them out there saving themselves for him while he's out running around.

While Natali salivates over Redd, Donny and Joe-Joe come in one after another.

Like I said before, Donny handles the Bronx for me. He's six feet two, weighs about two hundred sixty pounds and doesn't have an ounce of body fat on him. With his smooth, bald head, he looks like a gladiator. Donny is a very intimidating sight to see.

He pulls in about seventy grand a week selling what he calls his big three—crack cocaine, purple haze and wet.

By the way Donny's looking at me, I think he forgot about the night I gave him the truth serum. That's a good thing. I don't need anybody knowing what's up in advance. But at least I know Donnie didn't pop David. That's enough to keep him in my good graces.

Joe-Joe's as gully as they come. He has to be to hold down BK the way he does. He's a five foot five powerhouse with a very daunting fight game. He coordinated all the soldiers in Brooklyn to help us trap and kill Salu's squad. No one wants to square up one on one against Joe-Joe. That'd be fucked up. A nigga would rather get blasted than take a gut shot from Joe-Joe. He's a damned beast.

Joe-Joe grosses between sixty and seventy grand a week. Like Donny, his biggest sellers are crack cocaine, purple haze and wet.

As always, Ricco strolls up last with his three hoochies. I don't know why he thinks he can show up fashionably late all the time. Ain't nothing fashionable about Karmela, Imisha and Pretti, his Italian, Thai, and Greek hoochie mamas, though.

Sometimes Ricco can be a pain in the ass, but I know now that David kept him on because he might be connected. I couldn't care less if his father is made or not. The half million he pulls in selling powder and crack cocaine, heroine, purple haze and wet every week is the only reason I'd keep him around. All the extra bullshit he brings to the table is way too much.

Joe-Joe immediately objects to Ricco's hoochies.

"If I woulda known it was like that I woulda brought Brittany," Joe-Joe hisses.

Brittany is a female bodybuilder who's always with Joe-Joe. I tease him all the time by calling her shemale and carpet muncher.

"No need to start trippin'," I tell Joe-Joe. "They're not gonna be in the room with us when we have the meeting."

"That's still fucked up," Joe-Joe replies. "The nigga knows we're tryna take care of business. This ain't no damned social get-together."

"Shit! Y'all know I got an image to uphold," Ricco says laughing.

"If you're so worried about your image motherfucker, how 'bout you not let niggas punk you and take your stash," I comment.

With that, Ricco tells his hoochies to leave. He watches them follow Natali out. I can tell he's real heated that I pulled his card right in front of his bitches. But, fuck him. I ain't got time for hurt feelings. I'm tryna do what I gotta do.

"OK y'all. If you didn't know that Ricco got jacked for his shit, you know now. Y'all got to be careful out there. You know mother-fuckers are tryna do whatever they have to do for a come up around the holidays. This is the time you need to be focused in the street. Don't let the bastards catch you slipping and shit. It's bad for business.

"What's fucked up though is how my scrawny-ass runner was able to deliver the down payment to me without no drama whatsoever. So how in the fuck did somebody let her go scott free for cash and decide to stick you up for drugs? The whole shit don't make no damned sense."

"Shit happens," Ricco snaps. "But it won't happen again. You can believe that. I'm paying you your cut on that package anyway so you don't need to be sweating it."

"First of all, I sweat whatever the fuck I wanna sweat!" I yell, rolling my eyes. "And second, you was acting like you weren't gonna pay for your fuck-up. The only reason you paid is Big Tony told your ass you had to."

Ricco looks at me like he's surprised.

"I guess your ass ain't know I was having lunch with him when you chirped me the day some punks took your shit."

"Well, it's over now anyway," Ricco says. He looks like he's heated as a motherfucker. His nostrils flare, and his face is red. I can tell that he hates the fact that he's getting played in front of everybody.

"Speaking of Tony," I start, addressing everyone, finally relenting some on Ricco. "I've arranged for protection in case my lieutenants start acting the fuck up. After all, I'm just a woman."

"Just a woman, my ass!" Joe-Joe says chuckling. "I've been with you long enough to see you flip the fuck out. You're ass gully as anybody sitting here. And you're probably a lot crazier."

"Be that as it may, I have hired guns at my disposal. Any time somebody tries to test me, they best know one thing. If you're thinking about bringing it, you'd better bring it right. There won't be any second chances. If you step outta line, you'll be dealt with with quickly. And that goes double for any of your soldiers out there on the street. I've been in a real foul mood, and I ain't about to be putting up with no bullshit.

"And one more thing. Just like with Ricco, if something happens to a package—it don't mean shit. I still want my cut. Big Tony still wants his cut.

"That's right. I'm blessing Tony for helping me out in my time of need. Any questions?"

"I thought we had an agreement," Donny says. "We don't fuck with the Italians, and they don't fuck with us. No offense Ricco."

"Fuck you," Ricco snaps.

"Anyway," I respond. "I'm doing what I have to do to protect my interests. If any of y'all don't like it, there's the door."

"Nah ma," Donny says matter-of-factly. "I'm gon' ride or die with you to the end."

"I'm glad you feel that way, Donny." I look around the room into everyone's eyes to make sure they're also in agreement.

It seems like it's unanimous. Even Ricco, with all of his sulking, isn't about to make any waves.

"Good. Now that you're all with me, I need to fill y'all in on something."

I tell everyone that it's time to move in on Billy. I let them know that I don't want to just take back the corners that Ken had. I want it all. The corners, Motherland Taxi, the whole shit.

I want Donny to get someone he trusts to hold him down somewhat in the Bronx so he can lead the assault. Since his shit is so thorough in the Bronx, I want Motherland to be operated from there after the takeover.

Of course there's rustling in the room, especially from Ricco. He likes to think that he's next in line after the generals. I can't let on that Donny's the only one I fully trust right now so I feed them some bullshit about nobody ever wanting to come up in the South Bronx.

Sarge and Rott don't care since they're already so damned busy in Jersey. Redd and Joe-Joe are the consummate team players, and of course, Donny is beyond stoked. This is like a promotion to him.

But Ricco is acting like so much of a bitch about it that he's pissing everyone else off.

I throw him a bone by telling him that he's to supervise the move of most of the shit from Harlem to the Bronx. He's also gonna supervise a small, satellite office that will remain in Harlem.

The little crumbs I give him calm his ass down but it makes everyone else look at him sideways. I always thought he acted like a baby. Now everybody thinks that.

CHAPTER FIVE

The Streets Are Talking

December 26, 2001

Donny

I don't really like the idea of the Italians looking over my shoulder, but if that's what Fatou wants, what can you do? I'm making money hand over fist with baby girl, the same way I was making money with David, so I'm the last person who's gonna rock the boat.

It seems like everyone else is wit' me when it comes to that except that damned Ricco. I don't know why he's acting like such a bitch about it—especially after he loses a package, if he did lose a package. How you gonna expect to run some important shit like taking over Motherland Taxi if you can't even hold onto a package? Ricco's slipping like a motherfucker right now and needs to check himself before he wrecks himself.

These last couple days of popping niggas from Motherland have been the truth. A soldier like me ain't happy unless I'm getting my hooligan on in the streets like the gangsta I am. Billy "Bad Ass", give me a fucking break! I'm about to shut his shit down faster than a motherfucker can blink an eye.

I guess that's why baby girl wants me to be the point man for this shit. She respects my gangsta just like I respect hers. She was a mean son of a bitch before David died so I know she's gonna be off the charts now. I wouldn't wanna choose to battle with half of these punk motherfuckers on the street. But Fatou—I'd stand back to back with her ass any day.

The whole borough was wilding out when I told them that we're gonna take over Motherland. Then when they found out that I would be the man and that shit with Motherland would be run right in the South Bronx, everybody was giving me pounds and hugs. I got a lot of love. Niggas are straight feeling that shit.

Everyone wants a piece of the assault on Motherland. My wild-ass niggas on the streets pulled a couple of their drivers out their cars while they were waiting to pick up fares. Then they made their asses walk home. I think the term they used was, "You ain't gotta go home, but you better get your punk-ass outta here while you still can."

To make matters worse, after they made them ante up their rides, they fucked around, driving the fares wherever they had to go and taking their money. That shit is straight gangsta!

With all the support I have in the South Bronx, I know Fatou is gonna be pleased with the way I handle shit. And I'm gonna make baby girl real proud. It feels good to be appreciated so I'm gonna do whatever I have to do to show her she made the right choice.

Redd

I'm happy that not too many people ride Motherland Taxis in Queens. That means I don't have to be too involved in that shit. I have too much to do right now as it is.

It is kinda foul the way Ricco was acting, though. Donny's gangster to the core so I know he can handle the shit Fatou wants him to do. And even if I thought he couldn't handle it, it's Fatou's choice to do what the fuck she wants to do. Ricco's always the one putting shit in the game.

I can't figure out how that motherfucker's breathing, though. He ain't in the hospital, and he ain't shot the fuck up. How in the hell could somebody just take a package from him? That's some straight bitch shit. Let a nigga run up on me like he's tryna rob me. He'll find his ass on a fucking t-shirt.

What I can't figure is where were those three bitches when his ass was getting robbed? He brings their asses to a top lieutenant's meeting but doesn't have 'em around while he's picking up a drop? Something ain't right with that bullshit.

And they swear they're the shit. Yeah, they're cute. I'll give them that. But they ain't got shit on Fatou or her girl Natali. Come to think of it, I may fuck around and have to bust Natali's skins. Matter of fact, let me call her ass right now.

"Hello," Natali says sleepily when Redd calls her.

"Yo, Ma, it's big Redd. What you up to?"

"Hey, Redd. I was asleep. What time is it?"

"It's almost lunchtime. So wake that ass up so you can come check me out."

"Where you at?"

"I'm in Jamaica, where I'm always at."

"How am I supposed to get there? My car's giving me trouble so I know it won't make it that far."

"Take the E train."

"The train?"

"Yeah. I'm kinda tied up right now and can't leave the set, but I'll take you home when you're ready."

"You seriously want me to take the train?"

"Hell, yeah. What, are you too good to jump on the train?"

"I'm just saying that if a man is interested in me, the least he can do is come and pick me up."

"Well, check this out. You're starting out on the wrong foot. If you're trying to be high post like that on day one, how the fuck are you gonna be acting in a couple months?"

"Excuse me?"

"Look, Natali, are you gonna jump your ass on the train or not?"

"You ain't got to be getting all smart and shit."

"Yes or no."

"Ughh! Where you want me to get off?"

"Get off at Suphtin and call my cell. You got my cell number, right?"

"I swear to God, Redd, don't have me waiting. If I jump on the train, your ass better be there."

"Just call me when you get here. I'll be there."

"Alright, bye."

Like I said, I'm about to bust Natali's skins. Let them other mother-fuckers worry about Motherland. I'm gon' keep holding shit down in Jamaica and fucking like a rabbit while I'm at it.

Sarge

I'm glad Fatou didn't want me and Rott to be involved with that Motherland shit. I'm real busy right now, getting shit straight in Rahway. And I swear to God, if niggas don't stop fucking up in Paterson and Plainfield, I'm gonna bust one of their wigs wide the fuck open.

Plus, I was thinking about moving into New Brunswick and Trenton. Before it's over with, me and Rott are gonna have half of Jersey locked the fuck down.

I guess niggas know better than to try to stick us up for a bag. Plus, the scrawny little bitch that Fatou has running for her can't be more than a hundred pounds soaking wet.

If you were going to stick somebody up, why not choose her? You don't even need a gun for her ass. That's some 'ole snatch and grab, strong-arm type shit.

Ricco better get his head together. Whatever's bothering him better get taken care of. There's too much money out there to be fucking up.

The first thing that's gonna happen if he fucks up in Harlem is they're gonna ask me and Rott to help. And that shit better not have happened in Manhattan. How soft would that have been?

All I know is I don't have time for this shit. If me and my brother keep shit up, we'll be making about a million a week in Jersey before it's over. I ain't tryna fuck that up for no bullshit.

Ricco better get it together. If I have to pull his coattail, I will.

Rottweiler

Word is bond. Shit is real sweet right now in Jersey. Since I opened shop in Secaucus and Montclair, I can never seem to keep enough product. Plus with what my brother's doing, we're holding shit down for real.

I just want shit to be the way it was when David was alive. And he hasn't even been gone that long. Niggas don't need to start trippin' yet. Give Fatou a chance.

It's not like she wasn't handling her handle before David died. She was basically running everything anyway.

No, I don't usually fuck with bitches, but if she's keeping me laced with cheddar, that's a bitch I want on my squad.

I'll never forget what Joe-Joe told me she did to that motherfucker on New Year's Eve. He called her a bitch so she popped him in the head with one of her high heels then said, "That's Miss Bitch." Joe-Joe said the shoe was stuck in dude's head when they walked away.

Who could doubt a gangsta-ass bitch like that? Only one person: fucking Ricco.

Ricco's problem is he always thinks he's a chief. His ass don't know how to just be a fucking Indian. Like Biggie said, more money more problems. That counts double for power. Soon as niggas know you're in control, they're tryna scheme and shit to take what you have.

I'd rather just chill and keep living lovely the way that I am right now. Sarge and I have New Jersey on lock, and we keep duffing more and more Luchiano. Like Don King says, "Only in America."

Joe-Joe

I'm surprised that Fatou wants Donny to handle the Motherland shit and not me, especially since I was the one behind weakening them in the first place.

But I ain't trippin'. Donny's my nigga. He's a straight soldier. Any one of us can hold our own. Well, at least I used to think that.

I don't know how the hell Ricco could get jacked. And with the amount of product he's moving, I know that was a hurt piece.

But, hey, I would feel the same way as Fatou feels. I'm not gon' miss out on my money just cuz somebody else fucked up. I would just be like, "Run me that cheddar," the same way she is.

I'm not totally out of the loop with the Motherland shit, though. They have a lot of cars in Brooklyn. We've been picking those motherfuckers off left and right, too. I'm glad cuz I never could stand Billy's ass. That's why I ran his ass outta Brooklyn.

The pussy tried to start up a set down around Brooklyn College near Flatbush. Needless to say, me and my peoples shot up the Avenue so much that he decided to take that shit to Harlem.

I don't know what's up with that Ricco cat. Billy woulda been ass out in my part of town. I guess it don't matter who your family is. If you don't stand your ground when somebody comes at you, your ass will get got on these streets.

Ricco

I can't believe Fatou tried to play me out like that in front of everybody. Now she probably has the motherfuckers thinking I'm soft or something.

I know what I have to do, though. I'm gonna step up so hard that nobody's gonna have shit to say except, "Damn. Ricco handled his business up their in Harlem."

I still say it's bullshit that Big Tony got involved with the shit with Fatou, though. Why should I have to take the whole loss?

His old ass is probably sweet on Fatou so he's doing her favors so he can get in her pants. Whatever his major malfunction is, he's doing me dirty. He should be looking out for me not her.

The whole Big Apple is going topsy turvy. Like, how in the fuck is Fatou gonna put Donny in charge of the Motherland shit and not me? Everybody knows that everything runs through Manhattan first in this city. That's another damned slap in the face.

That's OK, though. Let motherfuckers laugh right now. They'll see that I'm still the man up in this piece. I'm just having a bad week. But you can't keep a hustler like me down. That's all I know. And it don't matter how many people try to put shit in the game, I'm gon' always be on top.

People may doubt me, but I'ma set their asses straight.

CHAPTER SIX

Word to Mother

February 12, 2002

Fatou

Donny's been working wonders with Motherland over the past couple months. In fact, I have to slow his ass down a bit so he doesn't totally decimate the company before our connections in City Hall are ready for us to take it over.

Joe-Joe has been a big help with Donny as well. There's been none of that hating shit.

I have to admit, even Ricco has come through. But I can't allow myself to trust him right now. David's killer is still out there and as far as I'm concerned, Ricco's my prime suspect.

When I drugged Donny, he told me that an emergency came up and David called him after I left the Bronx that day. Turns out that Ricco was at David's house with him.

David was on the speakerphone so Donny heard everything —even when David told him to hold on.

David was about to make Donny a captain. He didn't like how things were going in Harlem. That's why he had Ken helping out. But, since we bodied Ken, shit started falling off again.

Donny said that David hung up the phone and didn't hear anything else of the conversation. But he didn't blame Ricco since he didn't think that he was man enough to take David out.

I agreed with that statement but David was caught by surprise. I don't know.

What I do know is that I have to be careful with the whole Ricco thing. At a minimum, he's at least partially connected. Otherwise, Big Tony wouldn't have had the power to make him pay me.

Ricco probably thinks that, for me, it's about the money. But it's more about finding out how true it is that Ricco's father is a made man. Now I know it has to be true. If it wasn't, Ricco would've told Big Tony to go fuck himself.

I hate being political and acting all delicate and shit. But I'm a smart girl. I do what I have to do.

I'm sitting in my car, waiting for Donny. There's only a shoestring staff left at Motherland Taxi so we're just gonna take one more person out, a nigga named Slim.

Slim is Billy Bad Ass's right hand man. He sort of reminds of Snoop Dogg. He's so tall and skinny. He carries a 44 Magnum similar to what Ken used to have, but word is he only uses blanks so he won't catch a major charge.

I'm thinking, these wangster-ass niggas! How the fuck are they running anything, especially something as major as Motherland Taxi. Salu is probably turning over in his fucking grave.

When Donny pulls up, I get out my car and jump in with him. We ride over to Motherland's office building.

Through casing the place out, I know that Slim will be coming back from lunch any minute now. He's fucking predictable.

The thing that I don't get though is how come such a pussy doesn't have bodyguards with him. You'd think four or five motherfuckers would give him an added sense of security. Still, his light ass walks around acting hard like a real gully nigga couldn't tell his ass is a phony.

Slim pulls up right on schedule. I get out the car and walk up to him. The fear in his eyes tells me he knows who I am.

He pulls out his forty-four, but I don't even flinch. My calmness has nothing to do with the fact that I'm wearing my bulletproof vest. It's just that I ain't scared of bitch-ass niggas.

Bang! Bang! Bang! Bang! Bang!

I don't even flinch. The nigga really does shoot blanks.

I steal his ass in the face for disrespecting my intellect like that. I wind up dropping him with one punch.

I drag him to the car despite the fact that my hand is pulsating. I must've hurt a bone or something. I'll have to put some ice on my hand as soon as I get a chance.

Donny and I drive off while Slim is still knocked out cold. We're trying to figure out where we're gonna go to put his ass out of its misery.

I wonder if they send punk-ass wannabee gangstas to purgatory for trying to act hard when they know they're not.

I don't care that no one knows where Billy is. When I get the OK from City Hall I'm gonna take his ass out, too.

So Motherland is basically an even more anorexic shell now. The only thing I have to wait for is time.

Before Donny drops me off, I tell him that I've decided to make him a captain. That'll give him the freedom he needs to do what he does in the Bronx and help out in Harlem as well.

Donny deserves it. I feel kinda bad now for doing what I did to him. But he doesn't remember so no harm, no foul.

He leaves me looking souped as hell. I have to admit, I feel kind of giddy right now myself.

Nothing ever goes totally as planned, but in this case, I'd say that things are working out fine.

A remarkable chill suddenly takes over my entire body. Since I've been in America, nothing has gone the way I've expected it to go. Every time I feel a sense of happiness or accomplishment, shit goes totally wrong.

As much as I hated Lama, and as much as the thought of me, the child, having a child petrified me. When I finally had warmed up to the idea, Patra tricked me into letting her give me an abortion. I didn't even know what that shit was! And to add insult to injury, I almost lost my life over it.

When I finally started to allow myself to love Lama, Patra turned up pregnant, time after time after time. That poured more salt on my wounds. I was told that I'd never have children.

When I finally found a way to take my mind off of Lama, Patra, that spoiled bitch Nefara and Fifi, by immersing myself in my studies so that I could get my GED and become a naturalized citizen, I passed the test but the school was closed down by the INS before I could get my credentials or any of the shit I'd worked so hard to get.

And when I opened my heart to David after keeping it closed for so many years and fell totally, head over heels in love with him, he was taken from me in the blink of an eye.

I'm sitting here after not having a period since before he died and hoping, praying, begging that the joy, the miracle, that I think is growing inside of me isn't taken away from me as well.

But I know that something has to happen. It's my karma, I think. Every time I feel good about something, every time I allow myself to believe that I'm good and special, something bad happens.

Before I know it, I start crying. That's fucked up because I'm close to the check cashing place, and I don't need Natali sweating me and getting in my business.

I try to get myself together by letting the tears flow freely after I park. No use trying to stop things from going their natural course.

When the tears finally stop, I feel relief. It's like a big weight has been lifted off my shoulders.

I walk into the check cashing place genuinely happy for the first time in a long time.

Our manager, Suzy, bless her little heart, almost tackles me as soon as I get in the door.

Damn bitch, I think to myself, *can't I just enjoy this euphoria for a couple seconds before you start piling shit on me.*

Suzy is about five feet three and a bit overweight. She has long hair that's brittle, but it's all hers. I wish she'd do something with it sometimes besides pulling it back into the nappiest pony tail I've ever seen, but I've seen enough baldheaded bitches to appreciate her natural locks' potential .

Suzy's face is somewhat cute but nothing a nigga would die for.

Still, I tell her all the time that if she took a little bit more care of herself, if she put on just a little make-up before she left in the morning, she'd do herself a hell of a lot of justice.

But she never listens. She always walks out the door looking just so-so, light years away from as good as she could look.

She should go to the gym and work out, tighten her midsection. Or maybe she should wear tighter clothes to accentuate her figure a little better. She could do something.

Maybe it's a self esteem issue. She's convinced she doesn't have what it takes physically so she's decided to throw herself into her work. That's a blessing in disguise for me, but I feel real sorry for her. She shouldn't live and die for another person's business.

But I applaud her effort so I allow her to bring me down off cloud nine and tell me what's gotten her all riled up.

She tells me that there's a customer waiting out front for me. I ask her why she didn't just let the customer know that she's the manager and can handle whatever it is. But the customer persisted on speaking to me personally. In fact, she's waited for close to two hours.

I ask Suzy why she didn't call me on my cell phone, and she tells me she tried numerous times. I remember that I had turned the ringer off. I didn't want my phone going off in the middle of the shit with Motherland.

"Oh well," I finally say. "Let's go out there and see what in the hell is this woman's problem."

CHAPTER SEVEN

Blast From The Past

February 12, 2001

I recognize Patra immediately, as soon as I glance through the thick, bulletproof glass.

What the fuck does she want from me, I think to myself?

Patra still has her impeccable figure, even after having six of Lama's crumb snatchers. Her tits are still bigger than mine and they look like they haven't sagged a bit. Her ass is still one of those padonkadonks, and her thighs look heavenly. But with all of that going for her, she still has no waist.

When she lifts her baby out of the stroller, her shirt comes up, and I notice that she doesn't even have any stretch marks.

I guess I can see what Lama saw in her. I've always been jealous of Patra's sexy ass.

I do fine with what I'm working with, but Patra matches my every physical attribute. In fact, if it's not a stalemate, the bitch wins on all accounts except for my gray eyes. But a nigga don't give a shit about your eyes when he's fucking you from behind.

While I'm sizing her up, she turns and sees me staring at her. Her eyes look so dark. She's in pain. It seems like she's been crying since Lama died at the Twin Towers on 9/11. I guess the crazy shit Mati was trying to tell me really came true.

Mati is Patra's aunt or cousin, I don't know which. I say that because Patra calls Nefara her cousin, and Mati is Nefara's mother.

Mati lived in the house with Lama, Nefara and me when I came here so I guess she still lives there. I really should know that shit for sure since Lama's been dead almost four months, and Mati's the only one involved with Lama who ever treated me nice.

Truth is, Mati did more than treat me nice. She took care of me totally. She fed me, bathed me and emptied the bedpans that I urinated and shitted in when Lama locked me in his room for months after Nefara bitched about me taking too long in the bathroom.

Mati is my American mother. She's the only one in this country besides David and Natali who ever told me they loved me.

I love her, too. That's why I allowed her to wake me up the day I had just come in from working close to twenty-four hours straight. She was talking some shit about I was the only one who could save Lama.

She said an elder prophet from our homeland said something about Lama being punished for all the things he did to me. Supposedly, Lama was to stay away from mountains since two large, metal birds were going to crash into the mountains and he would die in the rubble.

The shit sounds crazy as hell, right? Well, imagine how crazy it sounded to me after not sleeping for almost a whole day and after having a couple drinks. As much as I love Mati for all she's done for me, I was thinking that day that she was one crazy old bird that flew over the cuckoo's nest.

Anyway, if you believe in prophecies and shit like that, it is disturbing that two planes flew into the twin towers, and Lama died when the second tower collapsed on top of his cab. That's some scary shit.

As much as I came to hate him, I still didn't want him to die. I wouldn't wish for any man to leave six kids behind, orphaned in a world as crazy as this world.

Truth be told, as much as I hate Patra, I feel sorry for her. She has six children to raise and that can't be easy for a hair stylist, especially a stylist who works for greedy Fifi.

I walk out to Patra, slowly, uneasily. When we embrace, I can't tell if it's real or contrived.

"You look good, Fatou," she says, "Real good."

"Yeah right, bitch," I reply. "You know you always looked better than me and you still do."

"I don't believe you. But if it is true, it didn't stop Lama from chasing after you and driving himself crazy no matter how many babies I gave him. He always wanted you back. I was never enough for him."

"Why are you here, Patra?"

"I have always known where you were, but I did not tell Fifi or Lama. And it was not because I was scared that you would take Lama away from me. It was because I felt like one of us finally made it. I was so proud of you. I am still proud of you. It's just..."

"Just what, Patra?"

"I've always been ashamed for what I did to you but couldn't find the words to tell you. I am sorry, Fatou, but I was so afraid of your power and so totally jealous of you."

"Jealous of me? You were the one who was fucking my husband. You were the one who spent all the time with him."

"That is only because he loved my body. He loved the things I did to him. But he considered me a whore. You, he considered a princess."

"Why are you telling me all of this, Patra? And why now?"

"Because I need your help."

"You? You need my help?"

"Mati has control over who gets Lama's death benefits. And I know you hate me. You have every right to hate me. But you do have it in your power to change Mati's mind. It is only right. I have all of these children, and I am struggling. But Mati says you will get every-thing. She says that you have earned it. I am asking you to be rea-sonable, Fatou. You know I need the benefits a lot more than you do. You have everything that you need."

"I knew that some shit was about to happen to steal my joy. I just didn't know what."

"Excuse me?"

"Anyway. So this is all about money? Is that what it is, Patra? You came here thinking I give a shit about Lama's money?"

"That is my point, Fatou. I know you do not want it. I have been trying to tell Mati that you do not want it. She just will not listen."

"You are right about one thing. I don't want shit from Lama. But what makes you think that I would help you, of all people?" Patra comes close to me and grabs my hair and starts stroking it.

"Because you are a better person than I could ever hope to be. Because I wish I was you. Because I wish I had your life. Every painful thing you have been through, I would take all of it. Have you ever seen *The Color Purple?*"

"No. I can't say that I have."

"Well, just consider me to be Mister. But the thing is, I always thought that I hated you because of you. I do not though. I hate myself because I am not you. I could never be you. That is why I know you will help me."

She turns to walk away pushing her stroller but pauses at the door.

"Keep making me proud, Fatou. Keep making all of us proud," she says as she walks out the door.

I walk slowly move towards the door and stare at her as she walks away. When she's finally gone, I realize that I've always wanted to be her and she's always wanted to be me. The irony.

I pull up in front of Lama's door and everything comes back to me. This is a part of Harlem that I've always avoided. I never wanted to relive the pain that I experienced. I was so young, so tender, so pure. This is the place that turned me into damaged goods.

I lift my hand to knock on the door but freeze. Although there's no music playing, I hear the wedding song. It's played at the ceremony where man and woman become one.

I hear the music and tears start rolling down my eyes like I'm twelve years old again—scared and alone in this big place called America.

I know what time it is when I hear the music since moments after the last time I heard it, my father prepared me for my real wedding by ripping my tiny, young vagina to shreds. He turned his precious little girl into a grown, tattered woman—one whose heart was ripped beyond repair.

"Please, Daddy. It hurts. Please stop. You're hurting me!"

He must not hear me. His grown-up penis is tearing my little vagina apart. Daddy must not know what he's doing to me.

"Please don't do this, Papa Lama. Please don't."

"I'm not your Papa!" Lama yells. "I am your husband." He smacks my face so hard that my skin feels as if it's peeling off my face. I guess that was the exclamation point his words needed. I'll never reject him again.

"Come to me, Lama. Come and let me love you."

Lama is licking me, tasting me, touching me. I wish he wasn't, but I don't know what I am to do.

He's on top of me, pounding away, and I hate it. I have to find calmness.

My thoughts go back to the way my father caressed me. He touched me with so much care.

Lama is fucking me but in my mind I'm making love to my own father. I'm so confused.

I'm shaking. I'm hoping—no I'm praying—that Lama doesn't strike me again because I'm crying. My tears are so overwhelming that I'm about to drown.

I can't stop shaking. I can't stop screaming. I can't stop crying.

"Oh God, why me?" I'm scream at the top of my lungs.

"What is the matter with you, child?"

I open my eyes. There's no daddy. There's no Lama. There's only me and a face full of tears. I'm still shaking. I'm really shaking. And I'm still crying. I can't stop myself. The tears have control over me.

"What is the matter with you, child?"

The voice is Mati's. I feel her warmth. I feel her comfort. But I can't see past the tears. No matter what I do, I just can't see past the tears.

I leave Mati with tears still in my eyes. What was said is best left for another day. But I did tell her that I don't want shit from Lama. Whatever floats her boat, I don't care as far as his shit is concerned.

I feel obligated to tell Patra the good news, but I don't know why. She never did shit for me.

When I pull up near Fifi's, I wait a long time before I get out my truck. I'm still crying, and I don't want Patra to think that she had anything to do with it. I'm over that part of my life. I've been over it for a long time.

I can't bring myself to go inside Fifi's. I stand outside staring at Patra. She really is gorgeous.

I'm hoping Patra will notice me, but it's looking like she's caught up in her own thoughts. She doesn't have a client right now so now is the perfect time for her to acknowledge me so we can get this shit over with before she gets too damned busy.

I never noticed how beautiful Patra's face was until now. I guess the awful shit that her dark eyes are doing to her face right now is the contrast I need to make me remember her inherent beauty.

She reminds me of the girl who played one of the sisters in *Deliver Us From Eva*. She was also messing with Derek Luke in one of those motorcycle movies. I think it was called *Biker Boyz*. Anyway, I can't remember her name, but that's what Patra's face looks like.

I don't doubt that Lama loved Patra's body, but I wonder what she meant when she said he only loved the things she did to him. What did she do so differently from me?

She has three holes and tits and ass just like me. I can't imagine what she had that I didn't. I had enough to turn David's ass out.

The fact that Patra had something over me is like a strangle hold tightening around my neck. I never really thought about it before, but now that I am thinking about it, it's consuming me.

Since I can't get her to look my way, I finally hold my breath and walk in the door.

Fifi sees me and acts like she's seen a ghost.

"You no longer have a job here, child."

I guess that's the only thing her small mind can come up with after all this time.

"I don't need your money, Fifi. I don't need shit from you. I came here to speak to Patra."

"Hmm," she says rolling her eyes. "Well, she's still on the clock. She don't have time to be talking to you."

I can tell that butting heads with Fifi is gonna bring Patra trouble, and that's not what I'm there for. So, I quickly remember the only thing that can shut Fifi up is money.

"Don't worry. This is business," I say as I pull out three crisp one hundred dollar bills, ball them up and throw them at her. Then I look at Patra and say, "Back room."

I walk a few steps and realize that I want Fifi to feel cheap and unimportant, but I don't want her to play Patra out as much as I know she will.

"Wait," I say. "Give me one of those back."

"It's mine now, child," Fifi says stuffing the money deep down under her shirt and into her bra.

"Give me one of those back, bitch, before I whip your ass and take

61

all three of them then still take Patra in the back room." I realize that my fear of Fifi is totally gone. I don't fear anyone anymore.

She bats her eyes at me defiantly but still reaches in her shirt and pulls the money out. She holds one of the hundreds in the air, determined to win by making me walk over to her. I snatch the shit out of her hand, trying to pull her damn arm off in the process.

I walk in the back room and, of course, Patra is already waiting for me. She's looking like she's wondering what I want.

I try to break up the tension in the air by handing her the hundred dollar bill I'd just taken from Fifi.

"I want you to have this. Don't let Fifi know that I gave it to you."

"You are giving me money now?"

"I'm not giving you shit. You're about to earn this." Of course Patra looks at me sideways.

"Before we get to that though," I say, "I wanted you to know that I already spoke to Mati. I told her that I don't want shit from Lama."

"Oh, thank you, Fatou."

"Don't thank me yet. I stopped short of telling her to give it to you. You did me real dirty, Patra. So I couldn't bring myself to make your life easier after you made mine a living hell. It's up to you to seal the deal with Mati. I just put you on the right track."

"That is still more than you had to do. I don't know how I can repay you."

"Oh, you're about to."

"I do not know how. I do not have anything."

"You do have something." Still the curious look. "Let me put it like this, Patra. I used to drive myself crazy wondering what you had that I didn't have that drove Lama into your bed every night. I've been wondering about that all day.

"I didn't know what I would do or say after I left Mati, but I knew I had to come here. I didn't figure out what I would do until I stood there watching you from outside the shop. Even then, I didn't have all the facts straight. Everything came together, though, when I walked through the door and found Fifi was still being her charming self."

Patra laughs. She knows that I'm just being sarcastic.

"Well, you're gonna work for me, Patra."

"Work for you? I do not know anything about cashing checks. And, besides, Fifi would hunt me down and have me sent back to Africa if I left her hanging."

"Yeah, well, she didn't find me, did she? I know her ass wanted to stick it to me bad as hell."

"You're right about that." Patra starts laughing heartily. "You know, Fatou, I meant it when I said I was ashamed for what I did to you. I also meant it when I said that I was sorry. You never did accept my apology."

"For that, you have to give me time. You just have to give me time."

"So, what can I do for you?"

I look at Patra and sigh. I know I'm gonna have to spit it out. All the baggage I've been carrying around with me for years about not measuring up to her has to come out right now.

"I want you to show me why you had so much power over Lama. I want you to do to me what you did to him. Well, you can't do to me what you did to him cuz I don't have what he had. But you get the picture."

I'm being loquacious so I know she thinks I'm babbling on and on.

"Fatou, you're not a lesbian and neither am I."

"You're right about that but this is not about being gay. This is about healing old wounds. I never understood why Lama could leave all of this and run to you all the time."

I start undressing. I get somewhat annoyed that Patra is acting like she's not gonna let go down what I want to go down.

"I did pay my money for this, Patra."

"Why are you doing this, Fatou? I already told you I was sorry."

"This is not about you. This is about me. Are you gonna get undressed or am I gonna have to walk out of here unsatisfied, bitching to Fifi."

Patra starts pulling off her clothes and once she's totally naked, I have to admit to myself that her body is amazing. But, shit, my body's amazing, too.

I can tell she thinks the same thing by the way that's she's looking at me.

I get close to her so that I can smell her. She smells wonderful. She's definitely not the crabby little bitch I thought she was. She's clean, gorgeous and totally stacked. If I was a carpet muncher, she would definitely my type.

"I can't do this," I say. "Let me rephrase that. I'm not gonna do this. I don't think that I ever really planned on doing it. I just wanted you to feel how powerless I felt when your naked ass was all over my husband. Do you remember how much you used to gloat when you came back into the shop from this room? You were driving a dagger through my heart."

"But you hated Lama, Fatou."

"I hated him, but I loved him. Then I hated him cuz I couldn't have him the way you had him. If you added it all up, though, I loved him. And know this: when he died, I still loved him. I just didn't love him the way you loved him. How could I? He wasn't mine, he was yours."

She stares at me, stupefied, amazed at how the oppressed can love the oppressor.

I feel like women have been doing that shit for decades. If I had the answer, maybe I could make tons of women leave when they always choose to stay.

"Get dressed," I tell her. "You're leaving with me."

"What?"

"You are leaving with me. You're gonna work for me." Still the curious look.

"You've been making money lying on your back forever. It's about time you get paid for it. Lord knows you have skills. You had enough to take Lama out of my arms and into yours. I'm sure you'll work out."

"But what about Fifi?"

"Fuck Fifi."

Once we're fully dressed, I open the door and drag Patra out behind me, holding her hand tightly. I walk straight towards the front door without missing a beat.

"Where are you going?" Fifi asks, sounding like a puppy that's only barking loudly because it's too scared to really get close enough to bite you.

"Get the fuck away from me," I sneer while pulling open the door.

I pause for dramatic effect and walk out, still dragging Patra behind me. I leave Fifi's, finally regaining something I had lost a long, long time ago. Who would've thought that Patra would be involved in my sense of closure now that I have put all the terrible things in my past behind me?

CHAPTER EIGHT

You Can't Fight City Hall

February 12, 2002

Natali looks at me like I've gone mad when I bring Patra into the escort service.

"What the fuck is she doing here?" she asks curiously. "You've gotta be kidding me! Her? Have you fucked around and lost your memory, Fatou?"

"No, I haven't lost my memory. And watch your mouth in front of the kids."

"Speaking of kids, what are they doing here?"

"She had to get her kids while she could. She didn't even have time to grab clothes. If she tried, there was a chance that Fifi would've had someone pick her up. She can't go back and all they have are the clothes on their backs."

"Well, where are they gonna stay? They can't stay here. No offense, but her children definitely cannot stay here. We don't have the room, and it definitely ain't that type of party."

"I know that, Natali, but have some compassion. You're not the one who has a beef with her like I do. If I'm over it then you should-n't have a problem with it."

"You're over it? If you say so." Natali looks Patra up and down. "So what makes you think she has what it takes to handle our sophis-ticated type of clientele? That can't be what she's used to."

"Well, show her the ropes. If she took Lama from me, I'm sure she'll do fine."

I think about what I just said and it dawns on me that Patra's kids are in my presence.

"Sorry."

I walk away without giving her a chance to respond.

For the first time in a long time, I think about my parents. It's been years since I've left West Africa, and I still haven't allowed myself to forgive them.

In a way, I could be glad about what they did since maybe they really believed that I'd have more opportunities here in America. I mean, I am sitting on over four hundred million dollars. I would have never come close to amassing that type of wealth in Africa.

But to spring it on me the way they did when I was just a little girl can't be considered right. And I haven't gone a single day without wondering if what my dad did to me was necessary or if he had been watching my body blossom for a long time, just waiting for an oppor-tunity to sully me for his own twisted and perverted reasons.

Yeah, I have a lot of baggage. My parents, my marriage, my preg-nancy, my abortion and now the death of the man I was in love with. David.

Bam, bam, bam, bam...

Shit. I can't even think straight around here, I think.

"What the fuck do you want, Natali? I'm kind of busy." I wipe away the tears that have formed in my eyes.

"Patrick is here from City Hall. He says he has something very important to speak to you about."

"OK."

I perk up a little since I'm feeling like this is the meeting I've been waiting for for a long time.

Patrick said that he would get in touch with me to let me know when we could start the process of taking over Motherland Taxi. We've all but crippled them, so now would be the perfect time to get the ball rolling.

I look in my handheld mirror to make sure that I'm OK to be seen. My eyes are a little puffy, but you can't tell that I've been crying. Knowing Patrick, though, he'll be too damn busy looking down my shirt to give a shit about my eyes.

Patrick is about five foot four with freckles that look more like a bad case of acne. He's not really a roley poley but he is overweight. His light brown hair is changing to gray on him and he's beginning to go bald. He always combs the back of his hair over his forehead to hide his receding hair line.

He kind of reminds me of the Italian boy who lost his girlfriend to Wesley Snipes when Wesley's character decided to cheat on his wife in the movie *Jungle Fever*. But Patrick's a lot heavier and not nearly as cute.

Another thing I don't like about him is that he wears Brut by Faberge. What grown man wears Brut by Faberge?

If my mind wasn't saturated with thoughts of my screwed up life,

I would have known it was Patrick by the disgust in Natali's voice when she called me. She doesn't even try to hide the fact that she can't stand him.

I take a deep breath and walk out to greet him. We give each other a quick hug before he follows me back into my office.

Patrick barely sits down before springing the purpose of his visit on me.

"You have to start filling out the paperwork to take over Motherland Taxi." He hands me a manila folder that presumably holds all the necessary forms.

"Relax, Patrick," I say, but in truth, I am anxious to finalize the deal. "What's the hurry? I've waited this long."

"Billy is dead. I overheard a conversation between a police captain and a lieutenant from Violent Crimes. You have to get your application in before the people who handle municipal commerce matters take their heads out their asses and figure out what's going on."

Patrick is trying to be charming, and it's irritating the fuck out of me. But I can't think about how annoying he is right now. I'm too busy letting his statement about Billy sink in.

"Billy's dead?" I ask.

"Wait. There's more," he says.

I'm wondering if I'm about to catch a migraine. I knew things were running too smoothly, and it was just too good to be true. First Patra shows up out of nowhere and now this.

"Are you listening to me, Fatou?"

"Go ahead, Patrick."

"Well, it turns out that Billy was killed some time ago. And when the cops started showing his picture around not far from where they found him someone remembered that a guy walked up and shot him in broad daylight. The description was real similar to this guy I saw you with some time ago. He was an Italian-looking guy."

I know immediately that Patrick's talking about Ricco. Instantly I start blanking Patrick out. He's talking but I don't hear shit he's saying. My mind is working, trying to come up with a way out of this shit.

I'm not too worried about Billy's murder being tied to me. But I am worried about having to replace Ricco. As dumb as it was for him to kill Billy, he's salvaged his reputation and that's gonna go a long way on the streets.

"Are you even listening to me, Fatou?"

I remember that I'm still in a meeting with Patrick.

"Yeah. I hear you. But look. I need a favor."

"Anything for you, Fatou."

"I need you to stop talking like the guy you saw me with has anything to do with this Billy shit."

"But, Fatou, this is a murder investigation."

"Yeah, and? Don't bullshit me, Patrick. I know that you have the power to steer the cops somewhere else. Besides, how many unsolved homicides are there in New York City anyway?"

"There's plenty, but what's your point? How will it look if I'm trying to get them to turn their heads over a murder?"

"The fact is that the person I know didn't have anything to do with it. I can't have my business looking bad by people asking him questions. He's gonna be running the whole fucking Motherland office in Manhattan once I do take over. If everybody's looking at him for Billy, that shit will set me back months just trying to find someone to replace him. That's too much work. Just make the shit go away, Patrick."

"Don't get yourself so excited, Fatou. I may be able to help you. But for something like this, it's gonna cost you. I mean, it's gonna really cost you."

"What do you want, Patrick?"

"For starters, I want that pretty thing that told you I was here. But I want more. I want a lot more."

"Well, what Natali does with her body is up to her. But if pussy is all you want, there's a lot of it running around here."

"Don't try to play me, Fatou. I'll be doing you a big favor here. Yes, all pussy is pink on the inside but don't try to act like everyone is like Natali. She's special. So, I want her and something else. I just haven't figured out what the something else is yet."

I know Patrick has me by my bra strap. I need his help so there's no way around giving him what he wants. But selling this to Natali will be like trying to sell a Muslim a Pork Chop sandwich for a million dollars and trying to get him to eat it before sundown on Ramadan. The shit just ain't gon' happen.

"So, do we have a deal?" he asks me.

"Wait here," I say.

I start rubbing my temples as I walk away. I knew I was on to something when I mentioned that migraine shit.

"Fuck no!"

Natali confirms my suspicions by turning me down flatly before I even have a chance to get the whole statement outta my mouth.

"But..."

"No."

"This is for…"

"Hell no."

"It's business, Natali."

"They ain't create a fucking business big enough for me to fuck Patrick over."

"Lower your voice. He might here you."

"Good. That will give him a head start with coming up with some other shit. Ugh. Fucking repulsive."

I have to laugh at her. The expressions she's making with her face remind me of Q dogs when they're posing for pictures or doing a routine at a step show.

"He's not that bad, Natali."

"Well, you fuck him then. How 'bout that?"

The mere thought sends chills down my spine like a spider is crawling on me or something.

"He doesn't want me, Natali. He wants you. And you know that I don't do that shit, girl. I never did."

"News flash. I haven't done the shit since I started fucking with Redd. And if I did decide to walk down that road again it certainly won't be with somebody like Patrick."

"So what do you want me to do? If you don't do this we could lose everything. And I'm not pulling your leg, girl. We could really lose everything we have."

"So he's blackmailing us, and his payment is a piece of pussy?"

"That's not all he wants. But that was the first thing that popped into his mind."

"You need to find somewhere for your new bosom buddy's kids to go so she can start earning her keep. I'm not fucking him and that's that. But I am willing to let him touch me. She and I can do a threesome, but in the end the only person he'll be fucking is her. I mean it, Fatou. It's bad enough I'm gonna have to use Brillo Pads on my skin for a week after letting him touch me. But this pussy has Redd's name written on it right now. And there's no trespassing."

"Fair enough. If you feel that strongly about it."

"I couldn't possibly feel stronger about anything."

"Well, let me try to go finesse this shit."

I walk out and head back to Patrick. I feel like a mediator between two people who don't want to budge. I can make suggestions but neither person has to listen to me. They can just stick up their middle fingers and tell me to fuck off. Mediators must have ulcers. It seems like such a meaningless profession.

"OK, Patrick," I say knowing I'm about to try to gas him up. "I have a surprise for you."

"So she'll do it?"

"Let's just say that when you walk out the door to go home, you'll leave here with memories that will last you a lifetime."

He starts smiling from ear to ear. I'm hoping he keeps smiling when he finds out the surprise is not fucking Natali.

"I'll be right back," I say. "I have to go set things up."

Not too long ago, I bought the adjourning house. At the time, I didn't know what I was gonna do with it. I just thought it would probably come in handy. As I go to talk to Patra, I'm now glad that I bought the house when I did.

"What's up Patra?" I'm glad that I got to Patra before Natali did, too. I'm certain that I will break the news a lot better than Natali would.

"Hey," she responds casually without even lifting her head.

"We have a major crisis here, and I need for you to get to work right away. You and your kids will be crashing next door. Take a quick minute to get them settled. But I must stress that you only have a very quick minute...I'll walk you over."

I continue talking to her as she and the children follow me to what will be their new dwelling.

"You don't have to worry about anything cuz the place is already fully furnished. There's even a Playstation I system. There're snacks, too, so the kids will be fine for a while."

We walk in the house, and Patra looks around in amazement. I know she's never before had this much space to herself.

The place is just a quaint little brownstone, but I had been taking the time to decorate it. No one knows it, but this house and the war with Billy "Bad Ass" were necessary distractions to help me cope with missing David.

The floor is carpeted in beige to match the soft leather sofa, love seat and recliner. The coffee table and end tables are blonde wood. I bought a solid oak entertainment center and had a special 32" flat made for me to match the light wood color exactly.

The kitchen is small so there's no furniture in it. But the cabinets were just recently installed by Sears. They also dropped off a brand new Kenmore refrigerator with an automatic icemaker in the door.

I hadn't yet bought dining room furniture but Patra and her kids can make do without. But I did put brass-framed day beds and bunk beds in two of the three bedrooms. Matching dresser and mirror sets, carpeting, sheets and pillows are in the same color scheme.

The third room, I decorated like a child's room with the exception of the king size bed. There're pink fish hung up all over the walls that perfectly match the pink and white crib that's off to the side in the corner.

I can tell that Patra is overcome with either joy or guilt when she sees the plush accommodations for herself and her children.

"I can't believe this, Fatou," she says teary eyed. "How am I supposed to afford a nice place like this?"

"You have a better job now," I tell her. "And with that being said, you'd better come and get to work."

"OK. I'll be right with you."

I walk to the front door and wait for her. I'm sure she wants to have a word with her children.

I never thought about the babysitting thing. We'll have to work that out later. But they should be fine for a little while. Patrick doesn't look like he's getting much of anything sex-wise. He should be done in like three strokes.

When we return next door, Natali has already situated Patrick in one of the rooms. Of course she was smart enough not to go in there with him until Patra joined her.

As the three of them get settled, I go into the video room. There're hidden cameras in every room that feed into the video room. Natali normally monitors everything to make sure the girls are safe when they're working. But today, I'll be monitoring the festivities for different reasons.

I'm still curious about what Patra can do for a man that I can't. It's been eating me up for years, and I'm finally about to find out.

I chuckle when the three of them get naked. Natali looks like she's gonna puke after seeing Patrick naked.

Patra doesn't look too thrilled herself, but I can tell that Natali's schooled her on the dos and don'ts of what can happen—especially the don'ts. Every time it seems like Patrick gets too close to Natali, Patra moves in and puts his focus back on her.

Patrick's flabbiness is repulsive. I didn't think that a man could get stretch marks, but that's what it looks like from my vantage point.

Patra's being a trooper, though. Right now, she's leaning over him and licking on his hairy-ass chess.

I hear Patrick tell her to wiggle her ass, and she's obliging.

Patra's ass must be turning Natali on because she's behind her rubbing on it, and from time to time, planting wet kisses on it.

I don't watch porno movies so I've never seen a woman with another woman before. It seems kind of odd.

Patra doesn't act like she's gonna make a big stink about it, though. Actually, I think I hear a faint moan coming from her mouth.

She turns her head, unknowingly towards the camera, and it looks like she's totally disgusted but still operating with a purpose in mind.

She lowers her head to his stomach, and at that point, I know what she's about to do.

She puts his thing in her mouth, seemingly to arouse him, but when she releases it to lick its side, I understand that he's already aroused. So much for the saying that big things come in small packages. I've never known that a grown-ass man could have such a little dick.

Patra seems to be doing by herself what David used to push my head to get me to do. She's pulling and pushing her mouth up and down on Patrick's dick, which isn't a long journey.

If I were keeping score, I would say that Patra knows how to give a much better blow job than I do. Even Natali looks like she's taking notes. And I'm sure that bitch has skills.

Natali stops paying so much attention to what Patra is doing to Patrick and lowers her head back down to Patra's butt. This time, though, she goes in for the kill.

She starts licking on Patra's clit from behind. At first, it seems to catch Patra off-guard. She's not accustomed to having a woman do to her what's being done right now. But I can tell that she's accustomed to the way the shit feels.

She starts wiggling her ass quickly, and the faint moan that I heard before is now unmistakably audible.

The whole scene is turning Patrick on, and he starts making comments that let me know that he is indeed an undersexed, old-ass pervert who's finally getting himself a little bit.

By the rumblings he's making, I know Patrick is close to coming. Patra and I must be on the same page cuz she takes her mouth off his dick and sits on top of it.

She tries to ride the thing like a horse but his dick keeps falling out. With a little dick like that, that shit is bound to keep happening.

Somebody needs to create a big ass, reinforced rubber band so that when a woman gets with a man with a little dick they can put the rubber band around both of their waists so his pencil dick won't fall out.

Finally, Patra sits straight up on his dick in the position that gives the little thing its best chance to actually stay in her pussy. Then she starts doing this winding thing with her body that makes her look like she's in a Jamaican dance hall music video.

At this point, I'm adding to Patra's score. I use to think that I could get it in but this bitch can fuck for real.

It's bad enough that Patrick is already ugly as hell. But the ugly faces she has him making now is a huge testament to her skills.

At this point, I've pretty much thrown in the towel, and I'm about to leave the video room. But when Natali stands up, something makes me pause for a second. I'm glad I did.

Natali stands in Patra's face. So Patra grabs her ass and pulls her closer. She starts eating her pussy while simultaneously fucking the shit out of Patrick. The girl is a sexual beast.

The way her eyes look, I don't even know if she's aware of what's she's doing. It's like she's in a zone and totally oblivious to her actions.

But by the way I'm looking at her ass in action, and the sounds coming from Patrick and Natali, she's the only one who's oblivious. It's official. The bitch is a fucking freak.

I've had enough so I leave the video room, wet panties and all. I didn't realize until I stood up that the shit I was watching had my ass creaming.

I remember that it's been a few months since I've had a little bit. My knees are wobbly as I walk away, and I'm trying to convince myself that Patra's not the reason I feel this way. But I know for a fact that I'm lying to myself.

"Maybe I just need some dick," I whisper to myself.

The thought leaves my head as quickly as it entered it. I know that I don't even have any good prospects for getting myself some dick. And I'm not the type of person that just sleeps around.

I'm amazed at how Natali and Patra allowed themselves to just get into it with someone they're not even in love with. I guess it takes a special type of person to do that.

All of a sudden, a feeling of serenity comes over me. I realize that there's nothing wrong with me. There was never anything wrong with me. Patra is just a freak of nature. No one could ever compete with a sexual being like her. That's why Lama used to go to her.

Granted, I'm zero for two with the dick sucking thing. Natali sucks a mean dick, and I just witnessed Patra give her lessons. But so what? I'm just average in that department. A woman shouldn't be judged because she doesn't make the tournament of champions for giving blow jobs. A man doesn't think just about getting his dick sucked. Does he?

Oh well. I stopped worrying about sucking dick when I started making seven-figure money. The only reason I did it to David is because he wanted me to. A nigga should be glad that I let him smell this pussy let alone hit it. The mere thought of me going down on a nigga is a violation. The shit's totally out of bounds—flagrant foul—in my book. I ain't got time for the bullshit.

But I do need some dick though. And I need to handle that. But I better handle some more important business first.

More money, more problems. If it ain't one fucking thing, it's another.

CHAPTER NINE

Repercussions and Consequences

February 12-14, 2002

I have to take my mind off the fuck fest so I call an emergency meeting.

As I drive off, my pussy is still dripping.

Fuck. I could've at least changed my panties, I think.

I have to address the shit with Motherland and Ricco. I'm starting to realize why David always seemed so stressed out. There's never a dull moment when you're the leader of an organization. There's always a fire blazing somewhere that you have to put out.

I decide to hold the meeting in the South Bronx. I know that nobody important would be caught dead there if they could help it.

Since I know it will take the twins a while to come in from Jersey, I decide to ride to Central Park and walk for a few minutes.

The last time I walked around in the park, I was thinking about my GED and becoming a citizen. Now, that's the furthest thing from my mind. I guess your physical appearance isn't the only thing that changes with time. Your priorities change as well.

An eerie feeling seems to come over me. But come to think of it, I've been feeling kind of funny ever since I left Fifi's.

While I drive away, I keep looking back to see if anyone is following me, but nothing. Maybe I'm just skitzing.

No sooner than the thought leaves my mind, someone appears out of the bushes and grabs me from behind.

He has a ski mask on so I can't see his face, but he's the strongest motherfucker I've ever been in contact with in my life.

I kick and scream, struggle, squirm, bite his hand, but nothing. It's like he's a robot that can't feel any pain.

Before long, he puts a cloth over my nose and mouth. I don't know what the hell I'm smelling, but it doesn't take long for everything to go black.

When I come to, I try to make sense of my surroundings but everything is dark and blurry.

Eventually, it dawns on me that I must be in some type of electronics store. There are gadgets and gizmos everywhere.

My arms and legs are tied to a chair. There's a piece of cloth in my mouth and a handkerchief tied around my head to cover the cloth. I've been kidnapped, and whoever did it took extra care to make sure that I didn't make any noise.

I use my senses and conclude that I must be in the back room of the store I'm in. I immediately think of a way to make noise.

I want to lift the chair and hop but it's the heaviest damn chair that's ever been made. I have to come up with a better idea.

I decide to bend over to bring all of my weight to my lower body. Then I use my butt and legs to push the chair backwards.

When I feel something behind me, I turn my head and see that I've bumped into a rack filled with lots of electronic gadgets. Looks like the perfect noise maker to me.

I bend over again then rock myself back into the rack. I can tell that it's moving a little bit so I keep repeating the process faster and faster. When I feel myself going too far back, I pull myself up with all the force I can muster so I don't fall with the rack. I realize too late that I'm too far gone, so I throw my body sideways before I hit the floor.

The rack crashes onto the floor and clanging sounds reverberate throughout the room. I also hear someone say, "What the fuck?" from a distance outside the room.

I know it won't be long before I have company so I work fast. I untie my hands enough to pull them out of the rope but leave the rope on to make it seem like I'm still tied up. Next, I grab a metal pole and sit on it so the end barely sticks out. Finally, I maneuver the chair back on its legs and try to calm myself.

"What the fuck is going on in here?" I hear as a light comes on and big ass with the ski mask appears not far from me.

"I don't know. It just fell," I say. I know it sounds lame, but I'm hoping he'll buy it.

"Fuck you mean it just fell? The shit didn't just happen on its own. I guess you think I'm stupid or something."

It takes all my strength not to comment. Instead, I just watch the stupid motherfucker look around like he's one of the Three Stooges trying to figure out something his little mind is incapable of figuring out.

"Is everything alright back there?" a female voice asks.

I'm thinking that must be a customer so my plan is working.

"You better keep it fucking quiet," ski mask says, waving his finger at me.

He walks off without even noticing that the handkerchief is no longer around my head.

Stupid motherfucker, I think to myself.

Nonetheless, his stupidity gives me extra time to continue untying my hands and legs.

I tiptoe over to the door and place my ear against it. I can tell that ski mask and the female customer are the only people up front.

Logic tells me that I can probably just walk out since ski mask won't want to give himself up. But I already know he's severely stupid, so I'm wondering if I should test him.

I haven't been a punk since before I left Lama so I decide to risk it. I bang on the door hard a couple times.

"Yo, stupid! You locked the door. Did you forget that I'm back here or something?"

There's a brief silence before I hear footsteps. I move to the side of the door and lift the metal pole in case I have to smack the shit out of his ass.

When he opens the door, I see that he's again put on his ski mask. Even though she's not in view, I'm sure the customer can hear what's going on.

I throw the pipe out of my hand and quickly brush by him before it even hits the floor.

"You make me sick doing dumb shit," I hiss.

I walk a few steps until I see the customer then I act surprised. "I'm sorry, Ma'am. I didn't realize you were here."

Of course I don't wait for her reply. I get the hell outta dodge as fast as I possibly can. She could've called me a bitch for all I know. I probably would've just thanked her and kept going.

When I get outside, I think about peeking in to find out who ski mask is, but I decide against it. I start to walk away but stop dead in my tracks.

"This is David's brother's store," I whisper to myself.

As quickly as the words leave my mouth, I see David's brother rushing toward me.

"What the fuck are you doing out here?" he asks. "Bring your ass back in here so we can talk."

"Bite me!"

I continue walking away, ignoring the fact that he's following me.

"I'm not playing with your ass, Fatou. I told you to come here."

He grabs me, and I struggle with him. I don't have my purse with my heat and my mace in it. But I am laced as usual and looking good despite being locked up for God knows how long.

A cock-diesel-ass nigga starts walking by, smirking like he's had to grip up a few women in his life.

"It's not like that, my nig," I shout. "This pussy is trying to kidnap me."

Cock diesel slows down but still doesn't butt in. He's looking at me kind of funny though.

"This is between me and her," David's brother says defiantly.

"Fuck him!" I snap. "I know you know Joe-Joe. Joe-Joe works for me. You ain't just gon' let this shit go down!"

The words barely have a chance to leave my mouth before cock diesel springs into action. He rushes toward David's brother who's reaching for his piece.

FATOU PART II: RETURN TO HARLEM *BY SIDI*

I push him off balance so cock diesel can grab him. He doesn't have a chance to get to his heat before he's slammed against the wall. Of course he starts negotiating.

"How the fuck can you walk away with everything and not take care of my brother's family? You ain't right, Fatou. You're gonna give me what's coming to me."

"You're right!" I shout before punching the dog shit out of him. "Oww, fuck!" I forgot that my hand was already hurting.

Diesel grabs the gun from David's brother and sends him on his way.

"You better walk, nigga, before you have to crawl! The only reason I ain't do your ass dirty is I know you're my man's brother."

"This shit ain't over, Fatou," he mumbles while backing away. "I swear to you, this shit ain't over."

"Are you OK?" Diesel asks me.

"Yeah, I'm good. What's your name?"

"Hulk."

"That fits you. You're a big motherfucker." I reach out my hand to shake his. "I'm Fatou."

"Nice to meet you. I've heard a lot about you."

"Well, I ain't heard shit about you. How do you know my man?"

"David?"

I answer him with my eyes.

"Everyone knows David. He's the fucking man. He's been grinding as long as I can remember." He pauses. "Well, you know what I mean."

"That's alright. I'm trying to get over it. Well, thanks for your help." I'm about to leave then it dawns on me that I was jacked.

"Fuck! Those pussies took my fucking car."

"Are you alright, ma?"

"I just forgot that when they kidnapped me, they took my car."

"I thought he was just trying to kidnap you."

"Nah, I escaped. But the stupid motherfucker was trying to kidnap me again in broad fucking daylight."

"I can give you a ride if you want, but I have to go get my car."

"That's alright. I need time to myself so that I can think. But there is a way you can help me."

Hulk's eyes are saying "anything" to me, so I proceed.

"I could use a couple of dollars since the fuckers took my purse. I need it to get home."

"No doubt." Hulk digs in his pockets and peels off a couple dubs.

"Give me your number so I can get this back to you."

"It's cool, ma."

"Your chivalry is cute, but I don't need your money, Diesel. Just give me your number so I can bounce."

Of course he obliges then goes on his way.

When I jump in a gypsy cab home, I can't get the image of Diesel outta my mind. His body reminds me of the guy who was married to Stephanie McMann from the World Wrestling Federation. I think his name is Hunter or something like that.

He has the cutest, chocolatey brown skin. His hands are massive, and I think he was wearing at least size eighteen Timberlands.

And don't let me get started talking about his lips. He's a chocolate brother but it seems like he inherited those heavenly things from LL Cool J. I was waiting for him to lick the motherfuckers so I could ask him what else he could do with those sexy-ass lips of his.

I don't know how long I was unconscious, but I do remember being severely turned on before I went under. The last thing I need right now is for my pussy to be creaming while I'm trying to think.

I sincerely took Hulk's number so I could give him his money back, but I find myself thinking that I can use him for other shit as well. I'll have to speak to Joe-Joe to get the 411 on him.

"What the fuck happened to your clothes?" Natali asks loudly as I walk into the check cashing place. "And where the fuck have you been?"

For the first time since I evaded ski mask, I look down at myself. My clothes are dirty as hell and all ripped up. I'm glad that the business is closed. I wouldn't want anyone to see me like this.

"I was kidnapped, but I escaped. But don't start asking me a lot of fucking questions. I'm not in the mood right now. I need to get my head together."

Natali grabs me and hugs me tightly.

"Well, whenever you need me, girl I'm here for you. You know that right, Fatou? I'm here for you."

"OK, OK, Natali. Damn! I know you have my back. You're getting your clothes all dirty though."

"Fuck these clothes. I can buy plenty of clothes. I could never get my sister back if something were to happen to her, though."

I push her away gently and kiss her forehead. Now's not the time to be getting sentimental and shit. My head is already fucked up. I walk away from Natali and head upstairs to take a shower.

I damn near jump out of my skin when I get out of the shower. Natali is standing there holding a towel for me.

"I want to do something really special for you," she says. "Sit down."

She gestures to a chair with a folded towel on it. She takes the towel, and I sit down. Natali dries me off then grabs my hand and guides me into one of the bedrooms.

She has soft blue lights in the lamp and one of those meditation CDs is playing. I smell an aromatherapy candle. The fragrance is remarkable. It must be a new scent because I've never smelled it before. It's off the chain, though.

She gets me to lay down on the bed and places a towel over me. Before I know it, Natali is rubbing heated oil onto my back and giving me a massage. My girl definitely knows what I need when I need it.

Before long, I'm sound asleep.

I wake up to the smell of curry. I open my eyes and notice a tray of food in front of me. Just the smell of curry makes me think of David. We ate curried goat all the time.

"Sit up, Fatou," Natali says from across the room. "You must be starving."

I can tell that she's been crying. Now that I think about it, her eyes look like she hasn't slept in days.

"I've been worried sick," she says. "You've been gone for more than a day. I can't tell you how many times your lieutenants have called here. I didn't know what I would do if I lost you."

Natali bursts into tears. I motion for her to come to me, and I give her a giant bear hug when she docs. We cuddle for a few minutes, her with her head on my chest and me stroking her hair.

"I'm a big girl, Natali," I say finally, breaking the silence. "I get into things from time to time, but I always land on my feet."

"Fatou, things are getting really dangerous. I don't get in your business often but I know you have enough money. Don't you want to give this shit up and live a normal life?"

"That's easier said than done. Besides, I have to find out who double-crossed David. If I don't do this, I'll never know for sure."

"If you're six feet under, you'll never know for sure."

"If I don't know shit else, I know how greedy Americans are. No one's gonna kill me cuz no one knows where all of David's money is. And none of the lieutenants know shit about David's connections either. I'm the only one who keeps food on their plates. They can't do a fucking thing to me."

"I'm glad you're so confident, Fatou. I'm glad you're so sure." Natali walks away looking sad and defeated. I hate to see my girl like that, but I have to handle my business in more ways than one.

I eat the entire plate of curried goat. In fact, I don't push it away until I lick the plate. I must've been a lot hungrier than I thought.

I grab my burnout cell phone from off the table. Natali must have placed it there when I fell asleep.

I have to call Nextel and get that phone cancelled and order another one, I think to myself while scrolling through my numbers.

One thing about this game, you don't ever involve the police. If you get robbed, you just chalk it up to a loss and try to be more careful next time.

I have to make arrangements for fake IDs, credit cards, a new ride—the whole nine yards. This time, though, I'll get two sets of everything so I won't feel so naked if this ever happens again.

I reach Joe-Joe's number and chirp him.

"Fucks up, man?" Joe-Joe responds. He's so fucking gangsta.

"You know a Hulk?"

"Yeah, but fuck Hulk. You've been missing for a day. We need to handle this shit."

"I know that. I want Hulk to help me. But before I get him involved, I need to know what type of nigga he is."

"Hulk is good peoples. But your squad is mad tight. You don't need no outsiders."

"Well, if it wasn't for Hulk I'd still be missing so I gotta show him some love. It ain't nothing against y'all."

"Well, you know Sarge & Rott are still in the city. They're staying at some hotel in Manhattan until they here from you."

"Good, I'll fill you in later. One."

I hang up and call Hulk.

"I need you to go to the Magic Johnson Theater on 125th Street." I don't even say hello when he answers.

"Who the fuck is this?"

"The only bitch that gives orders in this city. Hurry the fuck up. You're already late."

I go to Hue-Man Bookstore and order a cup of coffee and large chocolate chip cookie. I sit near the window and start reading a newspaper so I can see when Hulk walks up.

I know it's gonna take him a minute since he comes from Brooklyn, but I didn't wanna stay around and be preached at by Natali.

She should know that I already have enough reasons to be down on myself with everything that's happened. Not to mention, it's Valentine's Day, and I don't have anyone in my life to share it with.

David used to go all out on special days. He was such a sweetheart.

There were always flowers, rose petals, expensive chocolates, and flowing bottles of Cristal. He made sure that I was never taken for granted.

And I can't even tell you how much ice he brought me. Jacob the jeweler knew David by name just like he was a famous rapper or something. My man kept me laced and didn't give a shit about what anybody thought.

Those were the days. Now, I'm sitting in a bookstore by my lonesome on a special day—the most special day of all for a pretty lady like myself.

Hulk walks towards the entrance of the Magic Johnson Theater and looks around. His body language tells me that he's not gonna go inside so I take a moment to size him up.

He's changed his clothes and has on some Roc-A-Wear khakis, a matching camouflage jacket and hat, and S dot Carter sneakers.

I feel myself tingling inside and know that I'm wrong. It's barely been two months since David died. But with all the activity my coochie used to get, can you blame me? It's in desperate need of a workout right now, and I'm sure Hulk is qualified to give it one.

I get up and tap on the window until he sees me. He smiles and strolls inside to join me.

"Have a seat," I say. "We can go next door after I finish my coffee."

"It's not even smoking. Your ass ain't beat for that damn coffee or you woulda gulped it down while it was still hot."

"Chill, nigga. What, you got someplace to be?"

"Don't you know what day it is? Every nigga should have a place to be."

"Interesting," I say feeling like I'm about to put my sexy face on. "So you're gonna rush away from a fly ass bitch like myself who just so happens to be alone on Valentine's Day."

"Yeah. You're a fly ass bitch, but you ain't my bitch."

"I just met you so I'm gonna allow you that one. But I'm gonna just say this once. Any nigga who ever uses the word bitch when he's referring to me has to deal with certain consequences and repercussions. Speaking of which, the reason why I asked you to come here."

"I ain't mean it like that. I only said it because you said it."

"Forget about it. You can just make it up to me later."

"How so?"

"Anyway...can we get down to business?" He shakes his head and looks me square in the eyes. I'm feeling the fact that he's not drooling all over my cleavage. "Joe-Joe gave you the thumbs up. He says you're a thoroughbred so I thought I could ask you to help me out with something."

"I hope it's David's brother. I never did like the way he talked slick about David, that no one was allowed to touch him. All you gotta do is say the word, ma, and I'm on it."

"A gladiator. I like that." I lick my lips seductively and try to control my breathing. My pussy is pulsating. But I'm not sure if I'm more turned on by the fine specimen in front of me or the fact that I'm about to get revenge on whoever did David wrong. My man's probably turning over in his grave right now. And to think that the nigga expects me to give him something. That pussy must've bumped his fucking head.

"So what's up, Fatou?"

"You're an anxious-ass nigga, ain't you?" I laugh. "Alright. Yeah. I do want you to take that pussy out. But that's not all. I may have a spot for you on my team. I just gotta figure out where I'm gonna put your ass."

"I'd love to be down, but you know I ain't been full-timing it for a minute. I help my niggas out if they ask me, but I'm tryna fight this bullshit. I'm cased the fuck up right now."

"What're the charges?"

"Possession of a firearm. And I was with Ricco when that shit happened with punk-ass Billy. I heard that the Jakes might be about to come at Ricco. I know those pussies are gonna try to add some shit on my jacket, too."

"Yeah. You do have to be careful."

"But careful ain't got shit to do with David's brother. That's a different animal right there."

"No doubt. But I ain't tryna fuck around wit' the shit."

"Ma, we can do the damned thing right now."

"I need you to do something else first. Did you drive?"

"Yeah. I'm parked up the street."

"Good. I need you to take me to my spot on 110th."

Something told me not to be dirty tonight so I'm surprised I'm jumping in Hulk's car without heat. I do have my mace, though. I'm wondering if big niggas like this drink mace after chewing on some glass to wash it down.

I know I'm skitzing, though. Joe-Joe wouldn't have co-signed for

Hulk if he was worried about him. I put the bullshit outta my mind and started thinking about more pleasant things.

CHAPTER TEN

Valentine's Day Massacre

February 14, 2002

We go into the house I'm letting Patra stay in, and I tell Hulk to sit on the couch. I leave him sitting there while I go upstairs to look for Patra. Her bedroom door is open a crack, and I hear the television.

"Patra," I whisper from outside the door. I hear her rustling so I try to calm her. "Don't worry, it's just me, Fatou."

"Come in. I am not worried, girl. I am used to being woken up in the middle of night. That is just part of living in a crowded house."

"Well, don't get used to shit like that. This is a place where you can be comfortable. I just needed something and didn't want to take you by surprise."

"What is it?"

"I'm gonna be in the basement for a little while. I wanted to make sure where your kids are."

"They are in bed. And even if they were not, they would not be up and down the stairs in the middle of the night. They will not go down into the basement."

"Alright. I'll talk to you tomorrow, girl."

I walk out of the room and pause for a second. I continue to be amazed that I'm being more than cordial to Patra. I have the bitch living in my house and everything and I'm paying her.

"Later for that shit," I whisper to myself.

I come back downstairs and tell Hulk to follow me. He doesn't ask a bunch of questions, and I like that.

We get down in the basement, and I smile to myself. I'm more than pleased with what I've done down here.

One wall has a silky soft leather sofa along most of its length. The opposite wall has two wine refrigerators on either side of a granite bar. In between those two walls is an immaculate daybed adorned with Satin sheets and lots of plush pillows.

I grab Hulk's hand and guide him to the daybed. I push him down then stand over him for a second.

"Don't you be catching feelings, nigga," I say. But before I know it, I'm starting to tear up.

"What's wrong?" Hulk asks. "And what do you mean by catching feelings?"

"Sorry, but this is my first Valentine's Day in a long time without David. Still, I've been having all types of urges lately, and I'm not about to go without on a special day."

I push him down on the daybed again, and he looks at me like he's beyond confused.

I know there's no reason to fuck around so I just start pulling my clothes off. I don't even try to get sexy with it.

"Take your clothes off, nigga, damn," I snap impatiently.

"What the fuck is wrong with you?" Hulk asks.

"Let me find out you're a big-ass homo thug," I hiss before unhooking my bra.

He looks at me like he's about to choke my ass so I say something to clean it up a bit.

"What do you care about what's wrong with me? You're about to get some pussy that everybody wants but nobody can have. Just go with the fucking flow, nigga. Shit."

I guess that calms him down. He starts taking his clothes off. His shit is ripped. Abs, chest, thighs—his whole body looks like one continuous muscle. It looks like the nigga's been locked up for twenty years.

How he got it to be that way, I don't care. All I know is I'm about to devour his ass.

I start rubbing and licking on his chest. It feels like a brick wall. But his skin offers the perfect contrast. It's soft as a baby's bottom.

My hands go south to begin massaging his six-pack. I love the feeling of a well-toned man.

Just that quick, I remember all the conversations at Fifi's about muscle-bound men with pencil dicks. Immediately, I reach for his dick, and, luckily, I'm not disappointed. Niggas call his ass Hulk but they could call him Horse.

He's packing about ten inches of the widest, thickest lady killer known to man, a big dick. I'm impressed. I'm very impressed.

At this point, I figure there's nothing left to do but ride the thing. As much as I like it raw, though, and as much as I'm convinced that I'm pregnant, I tell him to wrap that thing up.

He reaches into his pocket and grabs the biggest rubber I've ever seen. I know I'm about to give the thing the ride of its life.

I mount him and he fills every inch of me. I find myself gasping for air momentarily.

I'm glad that I cream all over him almost immediately. But that's still not enough to loosen me as much as needed for a dick like his. I only have a little more than the tip in me, and he's adjusting shit down there that's not supposed to be fucked with.

I start thinking about seeing Patra ride Patrick and feel myself getting bolder. I mimic her movements and instantly feel bolts of electricity going through my body. It's a rush I can't remember feeling before.

I have half of his dick inside of me and the pleasure-pain mix has me pulsating. It feels so good to be with a man again.

When I go for broke and take all of him, I can barely wiggle my ass. Orgasm after orgasm takes me to another world. I can't tell if I'm screaming or unable to scream. Sounds seem stuck in my throat.

I'm oozing my juices all over Hulk's dick. The sensation is heavenly. I've only felt like this once before. Yes, of course it was with David.

My orgasms take me back to a time when I was getting it regularly. Many a night I lay there with my tears dripping onto David's chest.

When I regain some semblance of consciousness, I realize that Hulk's chest has a puddle of moisture on it. But it's not from sweat. Once again, I'm crying.

The mere thought of the ritual I used to share with David brings me back to my senses. All of a sudden I feel like I'm about to throw up.

"I have to stop," I say matter-of-factly. "I can't believe I'm doing this shit. I have to stop."

"Is everything OK, ma?" Hulk asks, sounding genuinely concerned.

I snatch myself off of him, and I swear it sounds like the cork being released from a champagne bottle. I'm a complete wreck and a sniffling, snot-filled, teary-eyed fool.

"Calm down, ma. It's all good. We can just lay here."

Hulk is being so understanding and it makes things worse. If he was an asshole, I could have easily cursed him out and made him leave. But he's showing a tender side that most thugs don't show. I feel even more terrible that I brought the best out in Hulk this fast. Somehow, I believe I'm spitting on David's grave.

"Just relax, ma. Just relax."

Hulk puts my head on his chest and tries to calm me. He doesn't even care that snot is running out of my nose.

"I can't just lay here," I finally summon the strength to say. "I just did some nasty shit. I can't just lay here."

Hulk gives me a look that signifies he mistook my words. Since he's being so sweet, I clarify my statement.

"There's a chance that I'm pregnant. If I'm fucking over my man's baby, I'm the worst kind of bitch ever. That's just plain nasty."

I get up and grab my purse. I take out the Early Pregnancy Test that I've been carrying around for days. I run into the bathroom certain that I've allowed my hormones to do the lowest thing a woman can do.

"It's negative," I tell Hulk when I come out the bathroom a few minutes later. I've barely settled down, but I feel a little better about myself.

"Come lay down, Ma. You're shaking."

"You're not getting anymore ass so you can stop being such a sweetheart." Hulk's eyes show me that he's hurt that I'd even think that's what's on his mind.

"OK. I'll lay down with you for a few minutes but no funny shit."

"I wouldn't have it any other way."

Hulk reaches out his hand to me and I go to him. I wonder how long I'm supposed to mourn. I've lived a really fast and torturous life, but the fact remains that I'm only nineteen. David did so much for me that I have to protect his honor. But I'm a woman all alone in a strange place. I have to avenge David. I have to.

I doze off and wake up to a hard dick up against my ass. Hulk's not trying to do any foul shit since I hear him snoring. He must be dreaming about what I did to him.

I nudge him a couple times until he finally stirs.

"Hmm?" he mutters.

"What's that about?" I ask.

"What?"

"This?" I reach down and grab his dick. That wakes him up totally.

"I feel guilty about this shit, ma," he says backing away.

"Believe me, you've been more than a gentleman about this whole situation. I just lost myself earlier. It's been so long since I've been with a man."

"A couple months ain't that long, ma. Imagine how I felt when I did a five year bid. That's a long time to go without getting any."

"David and I were always so stressed. We shared a lot and sex took the stress away. But it did play a major role in our relationship. Now I have to deal with everything I dealt with when David was here and then some, and I have nothing to take the edge off. In a strange sort of way, I know David's looking down on me, letting me know that it's OK. He knows how much I need this right now."

"And if I give you some more of this dick, then what?"

"Then we get up, wash our asses, and pay David's brother a little visit. We don't have time to get sentimental."

Hulk scoots back over to the middle of the bed. I mount him again and finish what I started. I'm in the midst of an orgasm, though, before I realize that I forgot to make him wear a rubber. I wish I had time to come off of my cloud, but I don't. While I'm coming, I feel his semen gush up inside of me. I bend over with my chest heaving on his. Another tiny teardrop falls down my face. I'm wondering if it's for David or for the shit I hope I didn't just get myself into.

Hulk and I wash up in the bathroom then head to Brooklyn. This time, I'm fully strapped and ready to handle my handle.

It's dark as hell in front of David's brother's store. As always, the street lights in the area aren't working. This is perfect for me since I have excellent night vision, just like a cat.

I decide to stay in the car locked and loaded while Hulk goes to the back of the store. The plan is for Hulk to flush everyone outside and for me to blast their asses.

Hulk is gone for about five minutes before I see him running towards me. He hunches down behind the car and before I can get a chance to ask him why he isn't guarding the back, the front door opens. We start blasting everyone one by one as they leave the store.

I don't know who the other two clowns are with David's brother and ski mask, but they catch it just like anyone else who just happened to be on the wrong damn team.

Hulk jumps back in the car, and we ride away looking around to make sure no one has seen us.

Before Hulk drops me off I ask him what happened. He tells me that he started a fire at the back door to make sure they couldn't leave out the back.

"Nigga, don't you know that the city could care fucking less about a couple niggas shooting each other up, but they'll put everything behind finding out who destroys one of the buildings they collect taxes on? And it's a business no less. Great! Fucking arson!"

"It'll be alright, ma."

"Well, step one is to get rid of this fucking car. Take it somewhere and burn it. Matter fact, drive down to Philly or Delaware, take the tags off and burn the fucking thing. Here's some loot to hold you over. Take Amtrak back. And don't say shit to anybody."

I hand him a couple gees and leave the car. He's trying to say something to me but I ignore him and walk away.

"Damn! And I couldn't even get any more dick tonight with his dumb ass. What the fuck can happen next?"

I go inside my business and relax in one of the rooms. My adrenaline is flowing too quickly for me to fall asleep so I turn on the television. I'm not really beat for reporters and the cruel things they're trying to tell me about the world, but every channel I turn to is showing breaking news.

Feeling defeated, I'm about to turn the television off, but the fire trucks I see behind the reporter make me pause. I turn up the volume so I can hear what he's saying.

"No one seems to know how the blaze started, but we do know that it's destroyed four adjacent brownstones in Brooklyn. Firefighters aren't ruling out foul play in what they are calling the Saint Valentine's Day Massacre. Over ten people have been found dead so far and several others have been taken to the hospital to be treated for smoke inhalation. As firemen continue to evacuate the nearby properties, we hope that they don't find additional carnage."

I don't know who this guy Murphy is that everybody talks about but I have a greater appreciation for his law. Lately, everything that could possibly go wrong in my life has gone completely haywire— sugar to shit for sure.

All I wanted to do was to smoke out the motherfuckers who kidnapped me and disrespected David. But due to Hulk's stupidity, my squad's work is on every damned channel in New York.

The cops must know it's arson. Why else would the reporter not mention that four people were found shot dead right outside one of the blazing brownstones? I think that's what's called on a need to know basis. The cops don't want to give away their trump card.

I'm starting to feel the way I felt just before David and I vacationed in Kingston. I can't seem to come up with any logical reason why I'm staying in this game. I seem to be digging myself a ditch that's getting bigger and bigger. Pretty soon, if I'm not careful, I'll be buried alive in the very ditch that I'm digging. I have to do something. I have to do something fast.

David's killer is out there, and I am closer to finding out exactly who it is. But I have to step shit up. If I don't, I'll end up being taken out instead of taking out whoever took me my man.

CHAPTER ELEVEN

Back to Business

February 16, 2002

I've been a nervous wreck the last couple of days. Word on the street is that police detectives and fire department investigators are combing Brooklyn, asking questions of everyone.

That's not my only problem, though. I went to my gynecologist to find out for sure if I was pregnant. She says the tests came back nonconclusive as far as my pregnancy goes, but that they're abnormal. She wants me to check into the hospital for a couple days to see a specialist who will run more detailed tests. I'm not beat, though. I don't have time right now to be in the hospital. There's a lot of shit I need to clean up on the streets.

Hulk came back yesterday, and I took him to get a new ride. I also gave him ten grand for his work and for keeping his mouth shut. Of course, I told his ass in no uncertain terms that he shouldn't think he's special just because I gave him some pussy. I'm not his girl, and he simply fulfilled a very pressing need for me at the time.

"If or when I want some more, I'll call you," I told him. "But don't start sweating me. We're playing this game by my rules."

He acted like he wasn't too cool with how I was talking to him. But I didn't care. I sent him on his way after he dropped me off so I could pick up my own new ride.

I'm sitting here now about to pick up a Hummer. They aren't as fast as I like, but they're built for warriors and that I most certainly am. One hundred percent warrior.

They don't have any in the color I want so I tell them to just strip one of the motherfuckers and paint it black. They try to talk me into getting a color I don't want, but I don't budge.

They say they're painting it right now, but I don't believe them. I think that they're calling around to other dealerships trying to swap. I don't know why men don't just listen when a woman says something. The only reason I'm sitting here calmly and not freaking out is because I know after they finish being dickheads, they're gonna end up painting one of the Hummers they have on the lot. I love to watch a man who thinks he knows everything eat crow.

I'm barely able to avoid the rush hour traffic when I get out of the dealership. I have to go from Jamaica to the South Bronx for a meeting with my lieutenants.

It's about 3:30 in the afternoon, and I hate being late. I told everyone that the meeting starts at 4:15 sharp, and I don't want to be the reason it doesn't start on time.

"Move that piece of shit!"

I'm yelling out the window, fueling my already excessive road rage. I know I can get a ticket for noise pollution but that doesn't stop me from blowing my horn. I have places to be and people to see. I'm ready to pop in my Ludicriss CD so I can tell people, "Move...Get

Out the Way."

I get to Donny's spot in the Bronx at 4:13. Immediately, I hate what I'm wearing. I had put on some tight black khakis to torture Hulk earlier, but I forgot that I would probably have to come straight here. The last thing I need is for my lieutenants to be looking at my ass, especially since I've been getting my weight back up over the last couple of weeks.

The heat's pumping in Donny's spot, but I decide to just unzip my coat and leave it on. No need to bring myself unnecessary problems.

Without wasting any time, I jump right in Ricco's shit.

"So, I guess since last time we met when I questioned your manhood, you had to go and do some stupid shit." I'm right up in his face.

"I did what had to be done." He doesn't back down. I like that.

"Can anybody tell me how hard it is for a bunch of ugly sisters to pick a pretty-boy Italian out of a line up after he shoots a nigga at point blank range in broad daylight in the middle of Harlem?" No one answers. "You did what you had to do. Give me a fucking break.

"Anyway, my connections in City Hall tell me that the police have witnesses. It's just a matter of time before they go after you, Ricco. So, we have to figure out what we're gonna do when they pick his ass up."

"No one's gonna talk when it comes down to it," Ricco says, defending himself. He's right. The cops are always complaining about witness intimidation in drug-related cases. But that doesn't excuse his stupidity.

"Ricco...honey. Please let me finish. I'm trying to stay calm so I can conduct a meeting here. Is that alright with you?"

I stare him down hard, and he doesn't blink. But he is smart enough not to open his mouth again.

"I really hate to do this, fellas, since the shit y'all have working in Jersey is amazing,: I say to Sarge and Rott. "But I need help. You can flip a coin if you want, but one of you needs to hold shit down for Ricco temporarily while he's dealing with this bullshit."

"I can do it," Rottweiler says immediately.

"Nah, nigga," Sarge protests. "What about your dogs? I ain't taking care of all them big motherfuckers."

"Them dogs ain't gon' fuck with you, bro."

"Well, they ain't gon' get the chance."

"I guess you're it then, Sarge." I interrupt them since everyone is starting to laugh about the shit, and I don't want the meeting to get off track.

"Sarge, I want you to mainly deal with Manhattan and only go up to Harlem if the new guy needs help."

"The new guy?" Everyone seems to ask at once.

"Oh yeah. Joe-Joe's boy. His name's Hulk. He's not a lieutenant. He's just helping out. He's a big motherfucker so the niggas who don't know him in Harlem won't test him. You just need to show him around a little, Sarge. You should be straight in Manhattan since everyone already knows you. Any questions?"

"Nah, I'm good," Sarge replies.

"Now, Donny," I continue, "Ricco can't really do too much with this Motherland shit until we're sure that his hands don't get dirty. I'm in the process of finalizing the paperwork with the city right now. It'll be just a matter of days before everything is in place. I need you back and forth between here and Harlem to make sure shit is tight. We have a lot on the line here."

"No doubt," Donny says.

"How's everything with y'all?" I ask looking toward Joe-Joe and Redd.

"I'm good," they both reply.

"I've heard," I say, laughing and looking at Redd. He blushes.

The other lieutenants give him shit for a little while before we get back to business.

"In front of everyone, Ricco, I wanna thank you for not having your girls with you while we conduct business."

"You only have to mention something to me once," he says.

"Good." I hand Sarge Hulk's number. "Sarge, give Hulk a call. If no one has nothing else, y'all can bounce. Everybody but Ricco. We have to talk about your case."

I'm impressed by how astute Ricco is while we're talking about Billy. He knows exactly how many people were around when he blasted Billy's punk ass. He even remembered their descriptions long enough to tell them to his boy who draws. He has sketches of them in his car with addresses written on the back. He had his people take the sketches and carry them around until they found out where the possible witnesses are staying.

We go to the drugstore, and I make copies of the sketches. I use my label maker to put their addresses at the bottom of the sketches. I don't want my own handwriting on the pictures. I give a set to Ricco and tell him that he should toss the ones that are written on. I also tell him that I don't think it's a good idea for him to have pictures of the people who could testify against him in his possession. We have no idea when the cops are gonna strike, and the last thing we need is a signed confession.

I reassure Ricco that no one's trying to replace him, but I think he should keep a low profile. It wouldn't even hurt if he took a vacation somewhere. But I'm torn about that since I don't want it to look like he's fleeing justice. I tell him that if he does decide to take a trip, he should pack lightly. That way, it won't seem like he's trying to leave for good.

"One last thing," I say. "Don't call me from your cell phone—even if it's a burnout. Maintain discipline. If you need me, call me on my burnout from a pay phone. And if the cops pick you up, don't call me. Call Tony. He knows how to get in touch with me."

"You act like I have a disease or something."

"If you do, you gave it to yourself. I'm trying to look out for you, but whatever you have, I ain't tryna catch it. You feel me? Give me a hug, man. Remember, low profile."

Being cordial to Ricco is the hardest thing I've had to do in a while. Personally, I think I did it to death. Maybe I'll take up acting when I get out of the game. He's the best lead I have concerning David's killer, but he's not gonna know it.

I meet up with Patrick on my way back to the check cashing place. All systems are go with Motherland. We'll be signing the final paperwork in a couple days.

I sit outside Patrick's office in my Hummer, trying to theorize how we're gonna handle Motherland. The Jakes are making it harder and harder to deal on street corners so we need a fleet of taxicabs to help push our drug business.

I decide to ride over to Motherland's offices in Harlem and talk to whoever's leading their shoestring crew. I don't wanna go inside since there could be one last, loyal, stupid motherfucker working there, dying to avenge his master's death like in an old karate flick.

I sit outside and wait for whoever looks at least somewhat business-minded to walk out so I can kick it to him.

At 11:58, an older, slim guy walks out holding a clipboard. He appears to be in his early forties, but his face looks stressed beyond his years.

"Yeah, he's in charge," I say to myself.

He's walking like he's in a speedwalking competition, but I get out and follow behind him. I catch up to him as he's about to go into a diner.

I introduce myself and let him know that I'm about to take over the company in a few days. I can't ascertain whether he has positive or negative feelings about what I've just told him. More than anything, he simply appears to be in a hurry to get back to work.

"It'll be nice to work with you, Miss Kone, but a couple days ain't helping me right now. You'll have to talk fast. I never take a long lunch. Lunchtime is always busy for us."

I find out that the man's name is Mr. Jeffers. He's been with Motherland for over ten years and isn't phased by a change in ownership. Through three different regimes, he's been able to keep his job.

He's a supervisor and dispatcher. He's not quite sure who he's working for right now but has been showing up to work regularly even after Billy was killed. He's been cashing out all of the drivers and handling everything. It's as if Billy was never there in the first place.

Mr. Jeffers makes me feel comfortable so I decide to go to Motherland with him after I watch him wolf down a turkey burger with lettuce, tomatoes, onions and honey mustard on a Kaiser roll.

I sit with him for about an hour and take about three pages of notes. Before I leave, I ask him if he minds if someone else sits in with him for about an hour. He doesn't care as long as whoever it is doesn't get in his way.

I shake his hand before leaving and go to my ride. I call Donny and tell him to change his clothes and meet me outside Motherland. I want him to look less threatening when he meets Mr. Jeffers.

After meeting with Donny, I finally go back to the check cashing place. I want to take a quick nap, but Patra has someone in the adjoining room, and she's working him out.

Having Patra on board may be the best move I've made for the escort service. Natali tells me that sometimes she has men lined up waiting hours to get with her.

I give up on the nap and decide to go to Long Island. It's been a long time since I've been there so I don't know how I'm gonna feel about it.

The house is a wreck when I walk in. I must've been really depressed because I can't imagine myself being so trifling. Still, I tell myself that I'll straighten it up after I take a nap.

I wake up between four and five, the witching hours for driving in New York City. I decide to clean up the house to kill time.

There're so many empty cups and glasses, it's not even funny. But I don't find any plates or bowls with dried food on them.

"No wonder I lost so much weight," I say to myself.

I check my watch and see that it's six-ten. Traffic still isn't as light as I would prefer so I pour myself a shot of Hennessey and start reviewing my notes. It's been a while since I've had a drink so I'm sure that it will have me feeling really mellow in a matter of minutes.

I review my notes of my conversation with Mr. Jeffers, and I know I'll be sitting on a gold mine. I can't believe that Jeffers hasn't been promoted to something more appropriate than dispatcher. I guess that's what happens when you get stuck working in a family business.

I'm gonna do right by Jeffers and give him a promotion. He told me that he never understood why Motherland didn't venture into Manhattan. He showed me statistics of how some companies are making money hand over fist in the downtown area.

Motherland and Gypsy have been staples in the black community. Other taxi companies ride by blacks and hispanics in Manhattan. We could definitely give Gypsy a run for its money.

Jeffers has no idea that Motherland stayed out of Manhattan because it couldn't do anything to bolster its drug sales. He had been left out of the loop and I'm glad about it. He seems like he is on the total up and up. He probably never even jaywalked before.

It's a shame. He's another example of how someone can do everything right and still end up not having shit.

I call Patrick and let him know that I need a small office building in Manhattan. I tell him that since it's for Motherland, I need something that will have suitable reception for the dispatch radio equipment.

After hanging up with Patrick, I call the supervisor who's handling building the dispatch in the Bronx. He starts to bitch a little about the time, but I check his ass real quick.

"And? Who the fuck do you think you're talking to?"

"I don't mean nothing by it. The old lady told me this morning to make sure I get in at a reasonable hour. She needs me to help her with something."

It's funny how the bitch comes out in a nigga once you pull his card. I'm sure he's heard more than enough about my work. Nevertheless, I tell him to take his ass home as soon as I find out that he can't answer my questions. I hang up with him and call Radio Shack.

I'm trying to find out if I can have the dispatch in the Bronx tied into the smaller one in Manhattan. Radio Shack can't help me with everything, but they are able to answer some of my questions. They tell me that I'll need to contact a more specialized company, one that deals with large communications projects.

I want Jeffers to run the dispatch operations, but I don't want him in the Bronx. If he's in Manhattan, his nose will be out of everything, and shit will still get done properly.

I'm definitely not gonna trust any of my wild niggas to handle a legit business. I'd lose everything to lawsuits because they went upside a motherfucker's head. Nah. It's not going down like that.

I end up not leaving Long Island until after eight o'clock. I actually handled being back here a lot better than I thought I would, but I'm not willing to push my luck.

I've come a long way in a couple months, and I want to keep the clear head I now have so I can accomplish everything I need to accomplish to get out of the game.

Like the Isley Brothers sing, "I Don't Wanna Be Lonely Tonight," so I take my ass back to Harlem where I'm loved. I may not tell her enough but being in Natali's company has helped me get over the hump.

CHAPTER TWELVE

Motherland

Late February 2002

Motherland is finally legally mine, and I have dispatches set up in Manhattan and the South Bronx.

Jeffers almost pissed his pants when I told him I was promoting him. He's in charge of all dispatching operations, and he has a staff. For his reward, he'll make six figures plus benefits.

I pretty much sent all the legit drivers to Manhattan with Jeffers. I kept a small number of them in Harlem and the Bronx just so we can put up a good front. But, for the most part, I hired a bunch of wild niggas to whip the taxis in the hood.

There are certain street corners cops who won't bother you. But for some reason, they go after others with a vengeance.

My plan is to have someone directing traffic on the hot corners and sending feens to our taxis.

I envision the scenario like this: a feen gets into one of our taxis, buys his shit, and jumps out after the taxi turns the corner. If the driver doesn't recognize the feen or if the motherfucker looks like Five

O, they act like they don't know what he's talking about and treat him like a fare.

All of the drivers know that if they get busted, they just have to eat the shit—make it seem like they're dealing on their own. They know to keep the company insulated from trouble.

It doesn't take long for our system to catch on. Even people who were skeptical about copping their hits are checking for us. Everyone has always loved our product but visiting the corners where we operated. Now we have the best of both worlds: all of our clients, Salu's and Billy's clients, our brains and muscle, and the best product on the streets.

We've exceeded our sales goals by five hundred percent the first week, and I have no reason to believe that the shit ain't gonna get sweeter. I can't wait for the first of the month to get here.

Good news travels fast. Big Tony calls me the day before Mother's Day, the first day of the month.

I can't say that Tony's a hater, but I'm certain he wants a piece of the action. One huge misconception is that people think that being a hustler is all glitz and glamour. They think everybody loves you and cheers you on. They couldn't be more wrong.

There's always someone coming at your neck. You barely ever get a good night's sleep, and your guard is up 24/7. Truth be told, I've been putting off seeing the specialist because I'm certain I have a bleeding ulcer or something.

I tell Tony that I'm too busy to do the restaurant thing today. I'm lying, since I'm no more busy today than I am on any other day. I'd just feel a lot more comfortable if he would meet me on my turf. I'm in Motherland Taxi's new offices in the South Bronx. I couldn't possibly have a bigger home court advantage than that.

Tony seems jovial as usual when he meets with me, but I can tell that something's going on in that devious mind of his.

He greets me with kisses on both cheeks, and, as always, he has his hand on the small of my back so he can pretend it's a mistake when it finds its way down to my ass. He's the same perverted old man I remember—still lusting after some tender, young shit he knows he can't handle.

Tony gets right to the point. He tells me that he and David had spoken before his death about our organization taking over Motherland but wasn't sure if I still wanted to do it after everything that's happened. Yet now that I have, he wants the same arrangement he says he made with David—ten percent off the top of everything.

I want him to define for me what he means by off the top. I won't agree to any skimming on the legal side of the business. Jeffers is on point, and he'll pick up on any funny shit quickly. Also, I don't want to be greasing his palms after I decide to leave the game behind me. When I'm out of the shit, I'm totally out of it. And I won't shed any crocodile tears if I don't see any of these motherfuckers ever again.

We go back and forth, but Tony finally gives in. Either that or he realizes that I'm not gonna budge about keeping his hands off of the legitimate side of my operations.

He departs feeling triumphant. The dumb fuck. I was willing to give up close to twenty percent off the top. If he wasn't concentrating so much on shit I wasn't willing to part with, maybe he could've fought for something that was attainable.

After I meet with Tony, I have a bad taste in my mouth. Every day

I find out that David told me a lot less than I thought he did. But I see no reason for him to hold out about the arrangement he made with Tony.

Now I'm wondering if I asked for help the exact person who set up my man in the first place. This playing detective shit is not as easy as it seems.

My day is flying, and I'm about to meet with Jeffers in Manhattan. He said that he didn't feel comfortable talking on the phone. But knowing Jeffers, he has some shit in writing to back up whatever it is he wants to complain about.

I'm surprised to see that he has stepped it up a little when I walk into the office. He used to have specks of gray throughout his nappy beard and wild hair. But now, all of his hair has been died black and his hair is cut neatly. Even his beard is shaped up.

I guess now I know why celebrities clean up their looks after being in the industry for a while. Money can do a lot for people.

Jeffers is about six feet one with a slim build and weighs about as much as Will Smith did when he portrayed Mohammed Ali. But his look reminds of the character named Smack Man in the movie *South Central*. He's quite attractive for a man his age.

When we sit down, Jeffers shows me all of these notes and charts about the Bronx office. He complains about not being able to speak to Donny as much as he'd like to.

He says he understands that Donny's managing the bigger office, but it's hard to be in charge of all dispatch operations if he doesn't have support.

I let Jeffers vent and don't try to steal his shine. He really is busting his ass for me. Everything is organized through his office, and the morale of the legitimate drivers is at an all-time high. Any driver I speak to tells me how they never thought things would be operated as efficiently as they are now.

I tell Jeffers that I have a lot on my plate and have to go but promise to take care of the situation with Donny.

I barely get outside before I chirp Donny on the Nextel.

"What's up baby girl?"

"Pay phone."

Donny calls my burnout from a pay phone five minutes later. It sounds like he's out of breath so I know his ass is busy.

"What's up Donny? Why ain't you making yourself available to Jeffers? You know he's the only person making our shit seem legit."

"I got a lot on my plate right now, baby girl. Those niggas in Harlem don't really know Hulk so I'm helping him stay on point."

"No, fuck that!" I snap. "He's a grown-ass man. He has to stand on his own two feet. And if he falls, he has to pull himself up."

"There's a lot of cheddar at risk in Harlem. Are you sure about handling it like that?"

"Let me worry about my cheddar and let that nigga, Hulk, worry about his own cheddar. It ain't doing nobody no good to baby his ass."

"Alright, ma. You're the boss."

"You're doing a good job, Donny, but I need you to spend a lot of time either at the dispatch office in the Bronx or at the satellite office in Harlem. That way, Jeffers can get to you when he needs you. Otherwise, he'll be wondering if your ass is ever at work. At a minimum, have someone call you and give you his messages when you have to step out. And call his ass right back."

"It seems like a lot of trouble to shut up some old-ass man."

"And you can die and come back to life three times and still not know half the shit he knows about the taxicab business. I don't give a shit how much trouble he is. His is the type of trouble I'm willing to deal with."

I bang on Donny and start my ride. I decide to take Central Park West all the way up to Harlem so I can keep my ears to the street.

I pass quite a few Motherland taxis as I'm driving. The whole time I'm thinking, mo money, mo money, mo money. I'm making it whether I'm coming or going.

When I get to the set in Harlem, I tell Hulk to take a ride with me. I know that I have to set him straight and don't have time for beating around the bush.

He catches me off guard, though, and starts on me before I have a chance to get him straight.

"I want to thank you, Fatou, for giving me this opportunity. I never told you how good it feels to know that someone believes in me."

"You'll be fine, Hulk. But you do have to step your game up. I need Donny to do what I asked him to do. He can't be spending his time changing your diapers and burping you."

"That's cool and all that, but he's the one who can't seem to let go. He's like my fucking shadow. No disrespect. I know he's a captain and all."

"Well, you don't have to worry about that anymore. I told him that I need his head in the other shit he's supposed to be working on. You, on the other hand, I gave you this gig because you's a big moth-erfucker. I need you putting your big feet up niggas asses or whatever you gotta do to check their chins. By now you should have the same street credibility in Harlem as you do in Brooklyn. Bust a couple of heads open if you have to."

"No doubt, ma."

There's silence for a couple seconds. I think he gets my point.

"Not to get on your nerves or anything...but can I see you later?" He sounds so cute.

I could get upset that he must not have heard me when I said we're playing by my rules. But my body wanted him the second that I saw him.

"I don't know. Maybe," I finally tell him.

I remain stand-offish. I know in my head that I have to keep the upper hand. But yeah, I want his ass. But I act uninterested.

"Alright. Get back to work," I tell him as I pull back up to his set. drove around the block several times while we were talking.

He gets out and walks away, looking as sexy as a man can possibly look. I know I'm gonna take him up on his offer later.

"Damn. I think I have a steady piece of dick," I whisper to myself.

With all the stress I've been dealing with lately, I know that I damned well deserve it.

CHAPTER THIRTEEN

Stepping It Up

March 2002

With everything going on at Motherland, and with me preparing to keep Ricco out of prison, I haven't been spending as much time on finding David's killer as I would like.

I meet up with my Italian buddies, and we decide to pound the pavement in Harlem and Manhattan to find out whatever we can. I'm concentrating on discrepancies between Donny's story and Ricco's actions. I'm not saying that I don't still consider Ricco my number one suspect. It's just that I don't want the culprit to get away scott-free. Whoever turned on David is gonna pay if it's the last thing I ever do.

I'm looking at my Italian buddies and feeling like I could've done a lot worse as far as warriors go. Frankie Rose and Jimmy Knuckles come highly recommended. Of course they don't use their real last names but who would in a business like ours?

Frankie was given the last name rose because it signifies red—the color of blood. If Frankie is around, you can expect to see something gory within a matter of seconds.

He kind of reminds me of a young Al Pacino—passionate, strong, and short. You'd better not play around like you're trying to bring the noise to Frankie unless you're real serious about your shit. When it's time to go there, he goes there on some straight gangsta tip.

Jimmy Knuckles is like a bulls eye waiting to happen with a gun but he prefers hand to hand combat. He received accolades as a Marine in Grenada but also kicked ass in Desert Storm until he got hurt. He was discharged on medical leave with a 60% pension. He has enough money to live comfortably, nothing too fancy. But that's not his style. Discharging a warrior like Jimmy from the military was the worst thing that the army could have done. I swear, he seems like the type who could have no legs and one arm and still crawl after you to tear your juggler vein out with his teeth.

Before the wars, Jimmy was a boxer. His record was respectable, too. His record in the military was eighteen and two. Both of his losses were by disqualification. When he snaps, he forgets where he's at and what he' s doing. That doesn't go over well when you have the strict rules of a boxing ring to consider.

After he healed, some of the connected family heard about his lust for the kill and recruited him. Back then, he hated guns. He preferred to beat a man's face in repeatedly until his nose, eyes, and mouth bled. I can't tell you how many times he's broken his hands. They're so swollen now it looks like he has two hands sitting on top of each other. I think it breaks his heart now that he can't tell someone that they're about to get a knuckle sandwich and actually follow through giving one.

I've known Frankie and Jimmy long enough now to fill them in on my suspicions about Donny. I also ask them what they think about the things Hulk told me about being babysitted. Depending on the answers that they give me, I may or may not tell them what I think about Ricco.

They do agree that it's odd that Donny's giving Hulk so much attention, especially since he's so tied up with Motherland. And it is common knowledge that on the street you have to hold your own. If you ain't strong enough to stand on your own two feet then you don't have any reason to be in the game in the first place.

They mention something to me about hearing on the street some time back peculiar things about Donny asking a lot of questions about the happenings in Harlem. That's seems odd to me since Donny has always been gung ho about the Bronx and pretty much acted like no other part of the city mattered. But what's even odder is the fact that Frankie and Jimmy argue over who told them about Donny. Frankie seems to think that Ricco was the first person who mentioned it. I could give a shit who Jimmy thinks told them. The fact that Frankie believes Ricco told them has piqued my interest.

"So, what do y'all think about Ricco? I mean, do you think he's been acting strange or anything lately?"

"Ricco's fine," they answer in unison.

"Yeah. He's a stand-up guy," Frankie adds.

I wonder if I should go where I want to go. I don't want to scare my best muscle away. But this is an opening that I have to pursue. I have to get to the bottom of things. I decide to push on carefully.

"So, if you had to choose between either Donny or Ricco to do some underhanded stuff, you'd choose Donny?" I ask.

"Actually," Jimmy says with the full weight of a suggestion I should heed. "If I was wondering if either Donny or Ricco was involved in something underhanded, then I'd come up with some other shit to think about. Maybe I'd think about wrestling a lion or something like that."

That was Jimmy's way of suggesting that I leave it alone—telling me to let sleeping dogs lay.

"I still get sad, you know? Sometimes I don't know if I'm just gonna break down in tears at any moment or not. I know I'm wrong for being suspicious, but I just miss David so much."

I'm hoping that a little modern day chivalry and understanding will steer Jimmy away from the fact that I'm asking questions no connected person wants to answer. I'm banking on the fact that showing the guys a little emotion and tenderness will allow them to see a vulnerable side of me that reminds them that they're men capable of relieving a damsel in distress of her pain. It seems to work.

"I know it's hard for you, Fatou," Jimmy says, pulling me to him. "But you're a tough cookie. You'll trip sometimes but you're the type of person who will always land on her feet."

"And with your looks, you can put your hooks into any man you want," Frankie adds.

"Yes, but David was special," I say.

"And you'll meet another special man," Jimmy says while stroking my hair and patting my back like I'm his niece or something.

"I don't know what I'd do without you guys," I say.

I feel victorious since I know I wiggled my way out of a sticky situation. I choose to quit while I'm ahead.

I decide to go back to Long Island so I can think. It's kind of early, and I know that if I go to the check cashing place, Patra's gonna be turning somebody out. I don't need to be exposed to that type of shit right now.

Once in David's house, I do something I haven't done in a while. I take the elevator to the attic.

I walk back and forth, looking at the monitors of the tunnels. I can't imagine how people who spend their whole lives down there feel about being stuck beneath the rest of civilization. Only a person who needs extreme amounts of privacy could stomach it.

I notice that the level of activity in the tunnels has died down in the months following 9/11. The number of crews has decreased dramatically since I last checked. I'm sure that my access to the tunnels will be renewed. The only problem is that with Underground gone, I won't have anyone to back me up in case I get caught down there.

I press the button for the safes to come down to the floor so I can get another look at about a fifth of David's hard-earned money — a hundred million dollars.

I wonder what I did to make my man choose me to leave his life's work to. What impression did I make on him? I never have to work again. I never have to dream or even think about working. If I wanted to, I hire someone to think about anything and everything for me so I'd never have to strain my own mind. David made sure I'd be set for life.

For that, I owe him. I owe him big time. I can't just sit back on my laurels and do nothing about what happened to him. Things are just so complicated.

Jimmy's warnings tell me that Ricco is more hooked up with Big

Tony than I'd originally thought. My only question is what in the hell does Donny have to do with all this mess?

And just think, I've promoted his ass to captain. I couldn't possibly demote him now. I'd tip my hand. I'm just so fucking confused. I don't know what to do with myself.

Since I don't have anything substantive on my mind or anything better to do with my time, I reach in the safe and grab a big wad of money. I caress myself with it for no reason other than I can.

How many people would love to be playing with this much money? I think. *None*, I think.

When I place the money back in the safe I notice a business card. I read it and discover that it belongs to Theodore Jackson, a private investigator who was murdered not long before David.

I start to wonder if David found himself exactly where I am today and tried to get more information before deciding his course of action. If he did, Theodore Jackson was murdered for it.

I'm feeling more and more like I'm treading in dangerous territory, but I have a burning desire to go wrestle a lion.

I close up shop in the attic and go watch television. Following my theme, I turn to a National Geographic special.

I don't see anyone battling lions, but there is a psycho on TV wrestling an alligator. I watch in amazement at how the man does something so dangerous of his own free will.

After the animal program goes off, a documentary comes on about people who do insane things because they don't have anything to lose.

I almost change the channel but the commentator introduces a story about a man who starts living dangerously after his insurance company cancels his policy once they find out he develops cancer. and cheats him out of the settlement his beneficiaries would receive after his death.

The man turns to a life of crime, doing whatever he can to make money and put it away for his family once he's gone.

My mind clicks with his dilemma immediately. It's funny how so much of my life revolves around television and movies. I guess that's what happens when you're neglected. All I seemed to do before David was watch television. So whatever happened to actors and actresses dominated my conversations. That's probably why David got me to watch all of Foxy Brown's movies as well as *Set It Off, Scarface, Menace I Society, New Jack City* and many others. He treated me like a pet owner who feeds hot sauce to his dogs. He wanted me to be mean, nasty, and prepared to attack. David wasn't worried about my brains. He told me all the time how smart he thought I was.

Well, not only am I smart, I also know when to take a risk. After watching the show, I decide on a certain risk I'm willing to take.

CHAPTER FOURTEEN

Suicide

April 2002

Last month was so up and down for me. I spent many nights crying myself to sleep thinking about David. But at least I wasn't depressed every night. I had my good days and my bad days. I guess I can't expect things to be any more acceptable than that.

One thing that kept me going was the amount of time I spent visiting hospitals and terminal care facilities. Yes, I fell off a little as far as making sure no one was shorting me with their kickbacks, but how much more money did I need to make anyway? I'm already set. All I thought about was justice.

I got an intense education about AIDS and the HIV virus, cancer, tuberculosis, hepatitis, heart disease, liver and kidney failure, and many other terminal illnesses. I never knew that so many blacks in America are infected with HIV, for example. We used to take it personally in Africa when the US did so little to stop the spread of the disease on our continent. Now I know that it wasn't about Africans. As long as people your color are suffering, the super powers in this world couldn't care less about you.

I know that sounds racist, but it isn't. Really, it's not about race. It's about wealth. People of color don't own most of the wealth in this world so they get shitted on. Whether you're Black, Hispanic, Mexican or Caucasian, if you live in a poor neighborhood, the powers that be don't give a damn about you.

I guess that's why Don Samuels looked at me like I was crazy when I knocked on his door on the Lower East Side.

Don is a private investigator who's been working in Manhattan for close to twenty years. He's an older, Morgan Freeman-looking black man with gray hair and a thin build.

I found out from a psychologist at the terminal care facility that Don has excessive kidney failure and won't be around much longer. The psychologist was concerned when Don stopped going in for his dialysis. She took it to mean that he was giving up on life and felt her pleas were being ignored.

Learning about Don seemed too good to be true. Since he's been working in Manhattan for so long, and technically Harlem is a part of Manhattan, he had to know about crime families

A private Jake with nothing to live for besides leaving a nest egg to his kids, who has twenty-plus years experience working the exact streets I need information about, I almost kissed him on the mouth the moment he opened the door.

At first he didn't want to let me in, but when you show a very sick, broke man—who depends on a thousand dollar a month Social Security check to get by—a fistful of money, he lets you in in a heartbeat.

He was trying to kick it big time, looking like he was wondering where in the hell I got my money from and how he could get more of it.

I didn't waste a second of his time trying to bullshit him. I told him that I knew about his terminal illness and that I also knew that he's a retired private investigator.

Of course he wanted to know why I was so interested in him and his life. I kept it real. I told him that it wasn't about him, per se. It was about helping me, and he could most certainly do that. And if he did, he'd be helping himself in the process.

That piqued his interest, and he asked me to tell him more. I didn't say another word. I handed him a piece of paper with names on it— Ricco from Harlem, Donny from the Bronx, and Big Tony from Manhattan. I made the list with my label maker. I also gave him a burnout cell phone before walking out. My eyes told him that I'd make it worth his while if he learned anything.

Less than a day later, he called me from the burnout and asked me if I thought he had a death wish.

My response was, "If you weren't terminally ill, I would've never contacted you in the first place. Think about your kids."

"So, if anything happens to me, my family will be taken care of?" he asked.

"Your family will have more money than you could have ever dreamed of earning in ten lifetimes," I answered.

He told me to give him a week and meet him at his crib. He told me that it was better to be discreet and not let anyone know that we knew each other. It could be dangerous.

He gave me directions to an apartment in high-rise building. He had created a hiding place to store information about the case. Whatever he found out, no matter how insignificant, he would put it there so if anything happened to him, at least I'd have it.

For that I promised to take good care of his family and instructed him to leave their names so I could get in touch with them.

That was a week ago today, and I feel kind of nervous driving back to the Lower East Side. I don't know what's in store for me once I get there.

Don's note tells me to follow up on his clues before I meet with him the same time tomorrow. He also asks me to leave some more money in the hiding place. No matter what else happens today, though, he promises to put anything else he finds in the same place.

I walk outside to my ride and hop in. Anyone else would have been nervous having in their possession incriminating evidence against important people in New York City's crime syndicate. But I'm not. I'm wired for sound I'm so hyped.

It doesn't hurt that I had bulletproof glass and tinted windows installed in the Hummer. I have also been wearing my bulletproof vest every day since the first time I went to see Don. I am in my own mini-fortress, eager to find out what making a hardworking family's American dream come true buys me in the Big Apple.

Skeletons are a big part of peoples' lives in America. In the motherland, if you do something, you own up to it and ask for forgiveness or redemption. Not here, not now, not ever.

In my country, we adore our men. We treat them like gods. I believed all men were gods until my father raped me.

In America, women have a love/hate relationship with men, especially black women dealing with black men. All I seem to hear is that men are dogs or men ain't shit. Yet all men can't be that bad. It must all boil down to skeletons.

For instance, if you meet someone and he tells you that he has no education, no chance for a decent living, bad credit, two kids, and a warrant out for his arrest for not paying child support, would you be trying to kick it?

How about if he dropped out of school to help support his sick mother and younger siblings, lied, cheated and stole, did whatever it took to get by while her condition worsened, married a bitch of a woman who gave him her ass to kiss every hour on the hour, put his younger siblings through college, and finally watched his wife run off with the boss who had him working twelve hour days earning a good living just because he knew one day, if he kept him employed, he may get the chance to fuck his beautiful yet conniving wife.

Same story, different perspective. Still in all, if you're the type of woman who believes all men are dogs, you probably hear scenario one even if the man was telling you scenario two.

For that reason, the skeletons men have stacked up in their closets remain there until they feel it's the best time to tell you about them. No one seems to trust in human compassion and understanding anymore. It's all about everyone wanting to keep his or her intimate details secret. If you give up the tape, you may end up catching a bad break.

But blacks aren't the only ones with skeletons in their closets. The president is at a minimum a recovering alcoholic. He probably had a drug habit as well. Former President Clinton got head in the White House but wasn't as concerned about finishing as Monica Lewinsky was. He also took some trees to the head but was ever so careful not to swallow the smoke.

You see, we're not out here on an island by ourselves when it comes to the skeleton thing. Hiding from embarrassing shit we've done in our past is multicultural in America.

I leave Don's place in the East Village and head to Harlem. I've been putting off telling Ricco about his indictment til the last minute but now is as good a time as any, especially with what I just found out.

I chirp Donny and Ricco and tell both of them that I need to have a private meeting with them about Motherland. We're scheduled to meet in half an hour, and I don't want either one of them to be late.

After hanging up, I chirp Frankie and Jimmy. I want them to be at the meeting with Donny and Ricco so I can lay it on thick. I'm the only person who can know everything. Everyone else has to be in the dark. So, if Donny and Ricco had any suspicions after our last meeting, I have to now put them all to bed.

We all meet at the Jamaican spot David used to take me to in Harlem called Rasta's. I'm certain that if anything were to happen here everyone would be sitting ducks except for me.

We find a quiet table far off in a corner in the back, and I ask the owner to dim the lights so we can have some privacy.

I don't even wait for everyone to push their chairs in before I tell Ricco he's gonna be indicted by the end of the week. I assure him that I've arranged for the best legal representation money can buy and hope he doesn't start worrying and getting sloppy.

I let him know that I don't expect him to work miracles since he has kept a low profile for the past couple of months, but I do still need his insight on the Motherland venture. I seek Frankie's and Jimmy's

134

advice on how he can remain productive in spite of the fact that the cops may start following him once he's indicted.

The entire time I'm speaking to the guys, I make sure to include Donny in the conversation as well. I look back and forth between Donny and Ricco as often as I can to look for similarities. But I don't want to stare.

They are all impressed that I'm so on top of things. They appreciate the fact that I seem to be getting back in the swing of things and leaving no stone unturned, no I's undotted, no T's uncrossed. If they only knew!

Afterwards, I go to the hiding spot but find out that Don doesn't want to meet me at his house. He wants to meet me in a safe place. I leave a note about Rasta's and tell him that I'll be waiting for him there.

He shows up two hours later looking totally paranoid. He thinks he's being followed and has been since he started using his sources to collect information.

I don't have time for the patient-therapist thing so I let him know that I want to get right down to business.

"I did what you asked me to do," I say, "and it does appear that Donny and Ricco are brothers."

"What do you know about the butcher?" he asks.

"Not much other than the fact it's rumored he's Ricco's father."

"Well, before the rumor started, the butcher was a nobody. Actually, he was just a fuck up trying to get connected who owned a real butcher shop, attempting to make ends meet."

"So, what does that have to do with anything?"

"Big Tony's the don right now, but he wasn't always. He was just a low level connected person, the object of affection for the daughter of the don at that time. Tony was very respectful and never crossed the line. But he was the only man who could make her happy."

"So the boss nudged Tony to pursue his daughter?"

He nods his head. "And they got married. Things were going fine until the boss's daughter got wind of Tony laying pipe to this bitch in the Bronx. But she wasn't just any bitch."

"She was black," I finally say, putting two and two together.

"Donny was born and taken care of sparingly. The boss didn't give a shit about someone in the family running around. He just didn't want to hear his daughter's mouth. He told Tony that whatever he did, he'd better not ever have another conversation with his daughter about some black bitch who lived in the South Bronx."

"So Tony forgot about his illegitimate child, and Donny grew up poor and neglected?"

"To a certain extent but not necessarily. Tony did give Donny's mom money but how much do you want to floss in the Bronx. They always kept a low profile. But that didn't mean that Tony wasn't still sneaking there to see them. Before long, Donny's mom gets pregnant with Ricco. At that point, the boss of the family is on his deathbed and makes Tony the don just to make sure his only child, his daughter and Tony's wife, is taken care of. That's when regular Tony became Big Tony and that's also when shithead Tony became Tony "the butcher"—on one condition."

"He had to act like he was Ricco's father."

"That's a skeleton that's been hidden in Big Tony's closet for years," Don says triumphantly. "But that's not all."

"You mean there's more?"

"There's a lot more. Donny's the real skeleton. He was just something that people never spoke about. Over the years, most people have even forgotten that he's Tony's son. But Donny hasn't forgotten. He hated the fact that Ricco got so many props just because he was brought up around connected people and knew how to play the game. Donny wouldn't know a thing about what it means to be politically correct if he spent ten years in charm school. That's why he stepped up to David the wrong way about the Motherland thing. He was incensed when he thought Ricco was gonna be a part of history, and he would be stuck in the Bronx empty handed."

"So Donny started making a stink?" I asked.

"It was a great big stink," he answers. "David was gonna reward Ricco for his hard work by making him a captain. Donny threatened Big Tony that he would let it leak out to the big brass from Italy that he was his son. Tony couldn't kill his own son so he suggested to David that he hold off promoting Ricco. Then he said that he'd heard many good things about Donny. There was a heated meeting about the whole thing between Donny, Ricco and David in the Bronx. No one seems to know what happened after that."

"This is a fucking soap opera. What about Donny following Hulk around all the time?" I ask.

"Donny doesn't just want Motherland, he wants it all. He wants the streets, the boardroom, everything he didn't have growing up in the Bronx pretending to be a nobody while Ricco was getting his shine on."

"So he hates Ricco for not living his life?"

"No. He hates everyone because he didn't get to live Ricco's life. He's a very bitter man who has the mindset of a child. And it doesn't help that his father is the most powerful man in New York City and has the ability to give him whatever he wants."

"Too bad I'm the most powerful woman in New York City, and I ain't fittin' to give nobody shit unless I want to. One question, though."

"What?"

"Why is Tony treating one son so much better than the other?"

"He feels like Donny deserves it and Ricco should be more understanding. He wants to make things up to Donny for his horrible childhood."

"Even if he has to hurt or kill a bunch of people to do it?"

"I didn't say it. You did."

CHAPTER FIFTEEN

Forgive and Forget

April 2002

After everything I've heard, I need to wind down before I do something stupid. I gave Don most of the money I had carelessly hidden in the basement of Patra's house. It was well over five hundred thousand dollars—not bad for a week's work.

I chirp Hulk and tell him to meet me at the spot. He knows what time it is. I know I'm wrong for what I'm gonna do when he gets here, considering that I'm still in mourning and all, but I have to admit that I'm damaged goods. My father and Lama took something away from me I'll never get back.

Now I feel like I'm just a sexual beast. Still in all, I've only been with four men in my life and two of them were against my will. That's something you can't easily get out of your head. You try to move on, but you know in your heart that it's not so easy.

When Hulk arrives, I apologize for being so distant. He didn't take it to heart. He says that he was busy enough as it was.

"What the fuck is that suppose to mean?" I ask. I can't believe I'm

139

acting jealous about the possibility of him throwing the pipe in another bitch's direction. He is cute as hell so I don't know what I'm thinking. His fine ass doesn't have to wait around for me to get my shit together.

I'm glad he ignored me because I couldn't think of a good comeback to his comeback. He just starts stripping while I licked my chops.

Yeah. That's the dick I've been waiting for, I think as it swings through the air in all its massive magnificence.

I approach him and start tongue kissing him. I could've easily gotten undressed but I want him to take my clothes off. There's something about the impatience and greed you see in a man's eyes when he's taking your clothes off that I really like.

He does so like he's a technician. I'm in dire need of his skilled hands to tune me up. Putting his other tools to work won't be such a bad idea either.

Once I'm totally naked, he starts licking my entire body like he's a hungry baby searching for breast milk. The thing is, he doesn't know where to find it—my neck, my shoulders, the small of my back, my belly, my inner thighs, or my burning, throbbing pussy.

Sorry, you missed a spot, I think, realizing that he has never sucked my nipples.

"I guess he wants cream, not milk," I whisper under my breath as he goes to work on my clit. I'm definitely about to give him what he came here for.

My cum shoots all over his tongue, face and chin like I'm a water balloon that all of a sudden busted. But I don't rest on my laurels or allow him to do so either. I want the rest.

I mount his dick while he sits on a chair and grind my pussy onto his entire girth. His ten inches is the tool I'm using to forget each and every problem I've had in this country. I'm putting my best foot forward.

The way he fills me is amazing. I love the way he puts his strong arms around me and makes me feel safe. Safety has seemed like such a fantasy to me in this country, but it doesn't seem farfetched when I'm with him.

He's palming my ass like he's kneading dough to make a loaf of bread. But I don't think he's ever felt dough so soft. There's a lot of junk in my trunk, and I'm working every last inch of it.

I don't know why though. I can't possibly allow myself to fall in love with him. I'm still in love with David and infatuated by the memories of Lama and my father. No, my father isn't dead, but both of my parents have been dead to me for a long time.

As soon as thoughts of my parents enter my mind, I make them leave. I'm really close to climaxing, and I definitely wanna get what I want from Hulk. This is one job I won't allow him to leave undone.

Then something happened just as I was getting in a groove. The doorbell rang.

I know that Patra is upstairs trying to rest but someone is laying on the doorbell, hard.

It isn't long before I hear footsteps. I know it's Patra trying to see what's up.

As I'm looking for my star after riding Hulk's rocket, I hear a knock on the basement door. It drops me back down to this cold, cold world. There will be no more orgasms tonight.

I continue to grind for a little while but once I realize that the knocker won't go away, I throw on an oversized t-shirt and go check it out.

I don't know why I'm surprised that it's Mati. I love her to death, but she always seems to be at the wrong place at the wrong time. She's fucking irritating like the guy who keeps poking you with his finger until you say something. I know that I've been fucking up, but I don't need her to be my conscience all the damned time.

She stands there with a cell phone in her hand and demands that I take it from her. It's been a long time since anyone has demanded anything from me. I have to think for a second about who she is.

I humor her by snatching it and get the surprise of my life. In an instant, all the air gets sucked out of my chest.

My mother is on the phone talking a million miles a second. I can barely understand a word she's saying. I rarely speak my native tongue anymore, and I'm finding it difficult to follow her words.

I'm finally able to figure out that my father is very sick. He wants to help me by coming to America so that his body can be used in case I need it for medical reasons. That sounds extremely peculiar to me until I realize that my gynecologist must have reached out to Mati. There's something to be said about a nosy person. They always seem to know everything about everybody.

I listen to my mom for a while longer before I finally lose it. Pretending is one thing, but I didn't want to hear shit about my dad and I told her as much.

"Fatou, why do you speak of your father so harshly?" she asks me.

"Oh, it's not just him," I say rudely. "I feel exactly the same way about you."

"But, Fatou, I'm your mother."

"You should have been my mother when my own father was raping me. Whose mother were you then?"

"Your father couldn't have raped you. We were always together," she says.

"Until you told him to take a piece of his little daughter's ass for a going away present."

There's a really long pause before I hear anything. Finally, she decides to speak.

"Fatou, I didn't know. You have to believe me. I didn't know."

"Are you telling me that you didn't want him to prepare me for my marriage to Lama and that you both lied to me about?"

"I sent him to talk to you...talk, Fatou, not touch you. I've never touched another man, and I never thought your father touched another woman."

"Well, I wasn't a woman, mom. I was a little girl. A fragile, scared, confused little girl."

"I can't believe it happened!"

"Don't worry, mom. It didn't happen to you. It happened to me. But you'll be happy to know that wasn't the worst thing that's happened to me since you sent me to fend for myself in this country."

"That was for the best. America is the land of opportunity."

"And believe me, I took advantage of each and every opportunity to drive myself insane. All I knew was how to be scared and pathetic. Well, I'm a different person now, no thanks to either one of you."

I can't take it anymore so I hang upon her.

Mati tries to calm me by rubbing my back and hugging me. She doesn't start right in on me, but I know it's coming.

I had forgotten that she was standing there when I broadcasted the facts about my troubled past. She must think I really am a walking nut case in light of what she now knows. But I can't worry about what anyone thinks about me. I have to be strong for myself, just like I've been for so many years.

"I understand how you feel," Mati says, interrupting my thoughts.

"No one can understand," I reply.

"You think that you are on an island by yourself, but you are not. You should never feel like your trials and tribulations are any greater than the next person's when you couldn't possibly know what they have been through.

"Well, if anyone has ever had to endure the craziness I've endured, I feel for them."

"Young girls in the motherland have been sold into loveless marriages for so long no one keeps track anymore. How do you think so many blacks ended up in this country in the first place? Children have made their parents lives easier for as long as anyone can remember, whether it's through selling boys and girls into slavery or selling girls for so-called dowries. It is wrong, but it is our heritage, and we have to be strong enough to get over it."

"I guess everyone has been raped by their fathers, too?"

"No. But you are not the first. And as sad as it is to say this, you will not be the last. But one thing people have been saying for years and years is that two wrongs do not make a right. You can never spit in your parents' faces then kneel down to pray to the most high."

"I haven't prayed in a long time. Praying used to be the only thing that got me through. I'd say, 'God please protect me from everything that I'm going through. Please take away the pain.' But I haven't prayed since my body was mutilated, and I almost died. I wasn't sure that living was worth it since I knew that I'd never be a complete woman again."

"You cannot curse God for these things. He has a master plan. Whether you know it or not, you are one of the strongest women I have ever laid my eyes on. You could not be anyway near as strong if it was not for your life experiences. God gave you extreme mental toughness to overcome the challenges you have faced. But after you conquer adversity, he will bring you many rewards. You cannot say that you have not been rewarded. Now you must repay the universe by helping someone who never helped you, by loving unconditionally someone who fell short on loving you in the same manner, and bringing hope to the hopeless simply because you can. Your strength can and will touch a lot of weak young people if you give them the blueprint on how they can be stronger. If you do not do that, your entire life will be worthless."

"Worthless?"

"Yes, worthless. God has put us all here for humanitarian reasons. If you are not going to live up to your responsibilities by letting your life be a living testimony to someone who is more scared than you ever were, how can you live with yourself? How can you look in the mirror at your pretty face when you know that inside is a cruel, vicious person I no longer recognize?"

"Don't say these mean things, Mati!" I tear up big time. I can't believe that she is talking to me like this.

"I held you in my arms before and tried to strip away the pain that was inflicted on you. Not because you gave me anything, but because I felt the need to give you the love and decency that every person on this earth deserves. And every time I turned your tears into laughs and your frowns into smiles, I buried a little bit more of the pain I carried with me about being sent to this country by myself as a young girl in the same predicament as you. It never totally leaves but a good deal has. Still, I hang onto some of it for inspiration. It reminds me how much I can endure the next time something is before me that is bigger than my abilities to cope. Hang onto some of it, Fatou, but let the rest go. As far as your mother and father are concerned, you only get one set, child. You only get one of each. If you cannot find it in your heart to trust someone you do not want to trust, why should anyone ever want to trust you?"

Mati walks away and both of our faces are drenched in tears. I never would have believed that she was a stranger in this country decades before I was. I guess that's why they say you should never judge a book by its cover.

As sweet a person as Mati is, I can't imagine her ever having the same feelings of hurt and rejection that I had and still have. She doesn't seem like a person with the self-esteem issues that come with being thrown out with the trash by your family. I guess that each day you're on this earth, all you can do is live and learn. All you can do is live and learn.

Hulk moving around downstairs reminds me that he's still here.

"God, what kind of can of worms have I opened now?" I ask myself, knowing that he must've heard a good deal of my conversation with Mati.

I walk downstairs without wiping my tears. There's no need. He already knows what time it is.

"I'm here if you need me, Fatou," he says.

"No, you're not here," I respond. "All you are is a fuck—a good fuck but a fuck nonetheless. I can't deal with anything else right now. Don't try to get in here," I say poking my head. "I'm like the heat miser, whatever I touch melts in my hand. Run away while you can, Hulk. Don't give me the chance to fuck up your life like I've done everyone else's."

The tears return, and he tries to be supportive by giving me a nice tight hug. I can't figure out why this stranger knows so much more about me than any other man. Not even David knew the entire story of my screwed up life.

Well, Hulk is the only one here so I guess he's it. No one else can console me right now. I just hope that he heard me when I said that he shouldn't start catching feelings and shit. If he does, it'll just be another problem I don't need right now.

The next day I set up a secret meeting with Ricco. I have egg on my face the whole time I'm driving to Rasta's. Even after I get there, I feel ashamed about how I've been treating him.

I can't believe that he and Donny are brothers. All along, I've been thinking that it's been him who's been acting like a little bitch. But it's really been Donny. Nothing's ever really as it seems.

Ricco walks in and for some strange reason can immediately see the pain on my face. He asks me if I'm alright, but I change the subject right away. He's not here to make me feel better. I want him here so I can be there for him.

I ask him if everything's OK between him and Donny, and he gives me the rote answer. His eyes tell me a different story, though.

I try to pick at him a little more by asking if he's still mad at Big Tony or vice versa. That opens him up.

"It's not the same, you know?" he says. "When I was younger, he was like an uncle to me—always looking out and treating me special. Lately, though, he's been kinda weird. It's like I've all of a sudden caught the plague, and he's trying to keep his distance from me."

I look at Ricco and think of some of the words Mati said to me. All my life, I've felt like my parents threw me away but at least I know who they were. Ricco has no idea. His whole situation is so sad.

I decide to delve further into uncharted territory. I choose to mask my intentions by leading in with an urban legend. At least, my question would seem harmless if he took it the wrong way.

"Do you ever speak to Tony the Butcher?"

"You too, huh? Everyone seems to think that he's my father. I shouldn't be mad, though. That's part of the reason that connected people in the city always treat me so good."

"Didn't you ever want to know the truth, though? Doesn't it eat you up inside not knowing for sure who your parents are?" I slip up and make a mistake. I hope he doesn't catch it.

"Maybe, but you learn to forget about it. And it's just my dad I'm unsure about. I've always had Jeannie."

Jeannie is the foster parent who no one ever really calls a foster parent. Donny's mother was instructed to put Ricco in a foster home so that no one would know. She could've either done that or been killed and then the state would've placed Ricco in foster care. Ricco's mother chose to be there for at least one of her sons, Donny. It's a shame the level some people will sink to insure that their skeletons remain in the closet.

I think again about Mati's words and zero in on her telling me that one day I'm gonna need to trust someone. I'm hoping, wishing and praying that it could be Ricco right here and right now. He must be in so much pain. I want to help wash it away.

"Before we go on, Ricco," I begin. "I have to tell you something."

"I'm all ears," he says.

"This won't be easy for me. No one knows all the shit I've been through in this country, and I've made it only because I've had to be tough all of the time. I never let my guard down. I hope it doesn't bite me in the ass today."

"I know you don't believe this but I've been loyal to you, Fatou. I've been loyal to you just like I was loyal to David."

"And he wanted to repay you by making you a captain, and I've been blind and fucked up everything."

"No you haven't," he says, defending me.

"As far as you go, I have and I'm sorry. And I want to make it right. Before we go any further, though, do you accept my apology?"

"Yes."

"No, Ricco. Do you really, really accept my apology?" I grab his hand and look him in the eyes.

"Why wouldn't I? I know you've been through a lot."

"You're so brave."

"What's that supposed to mean?" he asks.

Without answering him, I ask him, "Do you know who Theodore Jackson is?"

"I can't say that I do."

"Well, he was a private investigator killed gangland style not too long before David."

"So what's his story?" he asks.

"I can't tell you what his story is but I can tell you that the end of his story came as soon as David hired him to work his last case." I hand him the business card. "I found this in some of David's personal stuff."

"So, someone took him out over something involving David?"

"Can I trust you, Ricco?" I grab his hand and hold on tight again. "Can I really trust you?"

"With my life."

"I don't think you know what you're saying, Ricco. If I go any further, it may cost you your life. But things that have been blurry for a long time will start to clear up."

"If somewhere in what you have to tell me I find out you have my back, I'll definitely have yours. I'll be like a secret service agent who jumps in front of you when a bullet's fired."

"If I say anything else, and we don't have each other's backs, we'll both be dead. And I'm not talking about in a fallen-off-dead sense. I mean we'll be six feet under with cold skin."

"I feel you. But what's this about?"

"Forget about the butcher, Ricco. Tony's a good start but forget about the butcher."

"What are you trying to say?" he asks, looking really confused.

"I am legitimately concerned about your case, and I do need your input with Motherland. In fact, if all goes well in court, I plan to make you a captain. But none of that has anything to do with why I called you here the other day for our meeting with Frankie, Jimmy and Donny."

"Then what's going on?"

"I had to get a close look at you. Then I had to get a close look at Donny. Then I had to get a close look at both of you together."

"You're confusing me."

"Remember when I made a big deal about you and Donny sitting next to each other."

"Yeah."

"Well, I wanted to look at you both side by side. I had to see if the information was correct."

"What information?"

"Donny's your brother Ricco." I pause but not for dramatic effect. I want to see how he's taking it.

"Get the fuck out of here."

"I'm not joking, Ricco. But that's not all."

"You're serious?"

I ignore him.

"Donny's your brother. His mom is your mother, and Big Tony is your father. This is a secret that's been covered up for years. It's a secret that sent David to his grave along with the private detective named Theodore Jackson who discovered the truth."

Ricco's looking like he's searching his brain trying to make sense of my words. I can tell that many occasions of sitting on Big Tony's lap as a little boy are going through his mind. And the times when he threw his weight around to protect Ricco. He just never understood why Big Tony was doing it.

"Why are you telling me this now? And why would Big Tony hide this from us if it were true?"

"Because I thought you had something to do with killing David, and I was going to make sure that I murdered you myself. For being wrong, I owe it to you to tell you the truth. Those are my reasons. Tony's reasons are all about maintaining power."

"Power?"

"Yes, power that he never had without his wife's family. Getting his mistress pregnant and having Donny was bad enough. He knew that if the family found out about you he'd be x'd out permanently. A lot of people's lives were changed so that he could protect his secret."

"Like Tony the Butcher?"

"Or Tony the nobody. The fuck up butcher by trade who wouldn't have been shit if he didn't agree to spread a rumor that he was your father. The only reason he has a name today is because the old don did a favor."

"So Jeannie's not really my mother?"

"Your real mom is Donny's mom. Don't be mad at her. If she didn't go along with putting you in a foster home, Big Tony would have had her killed and the results would have been the same."

"This is all too much."

"It is a lot to swallow, right?" I ask him.

"How'd you find all of this out if Theodore Jackson died? I'm sure no one put this fiasco on paper."

"I hired another private investigator."

"So that yours and his days could be numbered?"

"No. I don't think that will happen. I placed five hundred thousand dollars in his hands along with pictures of everyone in his family. He's dying soon anyway."

"So what's next?"

"Well, I can't very well kill your father without your blessing."

"Don't you know how much backlash you'd receive if you did— even if you had my blessing?"

"That's why I'm the general and you're just about to be promoted to captain. I'll fill you in later. We have to get going to the airport. We can't miss our flight."

CHAPTER SIXTEEN

Road Trip

April 2002

The imagery in Italy is remarkable. The landscape is like something I've never experience before. There's so much history and tradition here. My only regret is that we don't have time to go sightseeing. We have a few hours to handle our business before catching the first plane back to the states.

Julius Bosco runs everything in Italy. He's the son of the man who handed over power to Big Tony. The only reason is that Julius's sister Francesca is the oldest of two children. Her father couldn't give her the reins so he gave the reins in America to Big Tony and made Julius the man in Italy. He's lived a good life, but I'm sure he's bitter about how everything went down.

For our meeting, I've brought old pictures, legal documents, birth certificates and social security cards and such, and additional other information Don supplied me to help plead my case. Even though there's bad history between Julius and Big Tony, I want to be prepared. Hate is one thing to Italians but money is an entirely different story. You can't come to them with something that's about to fuck up their money unless you have one hundred percent substantiated facts.

Julius has his goons pat us down. Once he sees that we have no weapons, I suggest to him that he may want to be alone to hear what we have to tell him. Italians don't take suggestions from women too well so I have to use my charm. Eventually he relents and it's just him, Ricco and me.

I've never been one for small talk so I kick things off by introducing Ricco to him as his nephew. We have a plane to catch. I don't have time to fuck around.

"Is this some type of a joke?" Julius asks. His English is impeccable.

"I don't know how much time I have left on this planet," I say. "But I do know that I'm going to use whatever time I have left to help heal old wounds. Ricco here has been hurting for a long time, and since he's been a good worker for me, I want the truth to be told. He has nothing to do with what has happened thus far. If you ask me, he's a victim in all of this. He's a victim and Francesca is a victim."

"What does he have to do with my sister Francesca?"

"His father was a bad boy. Too bad that it was only yesterday that Ricco learned who is father is."

"That fucking slimeball Tony?"

"You catch on quickly," I say, confirming his suspicions. "Many peoples' lives have been screwed up—or ended—so that Big Tony can hang on to his little secrets."

"Why do you say secrets?"

Ricco speaks up. "Because I also didn't know who my brother or real mother were until yesterday. They just happen to be Tony's son, my older brother, Donny, and the woman who has been raising him all his life. I've barely been able to say two words to her all of these years."

I can see the pain in Ricco's eyes as he speaks.

"You're talking about the black woman?" Julius asks.

"That would be her," I reply.

"Is that all?" Julius asks.

"I have some unfinished business to take care of," I say. "Once I'm done, I plan to leave the game permanently and have Ricco run everything." Ricco is surprised. "For his loyalty, and for everything that he's been through, I think that he deserves it."

Julius surveys Ricco with mixed emotions. I know all of this has caught Julius off-guard but he had to be more prepared than Ricco was. Everyone has had their suspicions about Big Tony all along. All I've done is to substantiate the facts.

"Nephew," Julius says and hugs Ricco, planting kisses on both cheeks. "Whatever happens, you will be protected. I can't speak for Tony, though. For him, I'll look the other way."

I take that as both a sign and an endorsement to do whatever we want to do with Big Tony. We chitchat with Julius for a couple minutes about nothing then head back to the airport. Coming to Italy wasn't a waste at all. I got exactly what I came for.

On the plane back, I fill Ricco in on why Donny had been acting like such a bastard. There's no pun intended using that word, but Donny did grow up living the life of a bastard child. Ricco's childhood was more stable and flashy. He had everything Donny always wished for.

It's hard to blame Donny, but like Mati said, at some point we have to heal the world, not make people suffer because we suffered. I feel her, but I won't start practicing that type of a Zen lifestyle until I get everyone who had something to do with David's death.

Ricco and I are both torn about how to deal with Donny. He has to have something to do with everything that's happened.

Both of us doze off before coming to any final conclusions. I guess Rome wasn't built in a day, and we can't expect to find all of the answers in just one day either.

We don't go straight back to New York. We decide to take a detour to Atlanta to give things time to trickle down from Julius to the rest of the family.

It's funny how being a made man works. When it's your time to go, you're always the last to know. It's like you're sitting there wearing a big dunce cap on your head that everyone else can see but you.

I have no compassion for Big Tony. Everything he is about to get he deserves. He's ruined a lot lives.

I go to Avis and rent a midsize car since I plan to go shopping. It has been a long time since I enjoyed myself by practicing my favorite pastime, shopping. I figure that I should at least do something I relish with the extra time I have on my hands.

Ricco and I have a helluva time finding the hotel since we get lost on all of the different Peachtrees. Every other street is named Peachtree Road, Peachtree Avenue, Peachtree Plaza, Peachtree Parkway or Peachtree Highway.

We choose to stay in the same room with double beds. I'm not saying that I don't trust him. I just feel better about him knowing where I am and me knowing where he is.

After we change our clothes, we get directions and have an easier time finding the Underground Mall. I said before that it has been a while since I've gone shopping, but it's like riding a bike. You never forget how. Ricco is amazed at how I've perfected being the consummate shopper and complains the entire time. I guess he wonders where I get the energy. Well shit! A woman can work twenty-four hours straight but soon as you say "shopping spree" she'll perk the hell up.

I have to soak my feet when we finally get back to the hotel. It probably wasn't a good idea to wear flats when I knew I would be shopping for hours. Flats aren't as bad as pumps but a better choice would have been either sneakers or Timbs.

After we rest, we go to Dave and Buster's to eat and entertain ourselves. We race each other on the large motorcycles, compete at basketball, ice hockey and everything else. We basically draw on most things, but when he challenges me to this gunfight game, I dig into his ass. We have a ball at Dave and Buster's. I am upset when they kick us out. I can't even bribe them to let us to stay.

I now understand why kids always fall out after you take them to a place like Chuck E Cheese where they can eat and play games. Ricco and I are pooped when we return to the hotel. It is barely eleven o'clock but we both fall into a deep sleep as soon as our heads hit our pillows.

After a couple of days of museums and comedy clubs and some of the best soul food I'd ever eaten, I finally get a call on my burnout from Frankie. He's the last person I expect to call me.

"Hi beautiful. How are you doing?" he asks, sounding more cheerful than normal.

"I'm fine, Frankie. How's everything going with you?"

"Couldn't be better. But I was dying to talk to you. Word is you wrestled a ferocious lion and lived to tell about it. I guess there's more to the thing about people calling you a princess than I ever knew. Take care of yourself, Fatou."

Frankie hangs up the phone. I understand that he was letting me know that it's cool to make my way back to New York. Word travels fast on the streets.

I guess I now know why Frankie was so staunch with me before yet pleasant today. I never did him wrong and always treated him with respect. It didn't hurt that I also put a lot of money in his pockets. I guess Frankie didn't want anything happening to the goose that was laying his golden eggs.

It's good to know that I can still count on him. I'm gonna need his ass when I get back to the city.

CHAPTER SEVENTEEN

Nothing But a Gangsta Party

April-May 2002

Ricco and I return to New York City, and he immediately turns himself in to the police. I've hired the best lawyers untraceable money can buy so I'm not worried. He's out of police custody before the ink even dries on the complaint.

I secretly start planning a surprise party for Big Tony. I invite every hit man I've ever hired—the ones I trust as well as the ones who give me the fucking chills. I have to stack the deck as best as I can.

I rent an extravagant hall and have it decorated to a tee. There are streamers and balloons and a gigantic Italian flag I had hand-knitted specifically for the occasion. Big Tony has fucked up so many people's lives that I want to make sure that I send him out with a bang.

I invite everyone Big Tony ever fucked over in his life. He's so arrogant, he'll be walking around with his chest puffed out instead of putting two and two together. I've never seen an ego as big as his. But all of it is about to end. Revenge is so close, I can taste it.

Getting Donny to take me to see his mom is tricky. Ricco can't let on that he knows what's going on, so he can't take me. I kicked some game about having a special event and wanting everyone who means something to me to bring their family. I tell Donny that I want to personally invite his mother.

Donny stays with us for a few minutes while we talk but things are getting too loud and he leaves. He doesn't want to be mixed up in our disagreement. It doesn't help that his mother is giving him dirty looks for even bringing me to her in the first place.

Once he leaves, I lay it on thick so that I can get her to change her mind.

"Believe me, you'll wanna be there. This is a special party for Big Tony and everyone needs to see him get the treatment he deserves." I give her a wicked stare, the kind that only a woman can understand. "Even Ricco will be there. Seriously, you don't wanna miss this."

Her eyes start to water so I know she's feeling me. I don't want to wear out my welcome so I decide to leave. I hand her a few hundred dollars before I leave.

"Buy yourself something special," I say.

The universe, or karma, always seems to have a way to work itself out. I've carried so much resentment in my heart for the people who've hurt me. But they all eventually met violent ends.

Lama was buried alive at the Twin Towers, and now Big Tony is about to be buried by his own web of deceit. As much as I hate my father for what he did, I never felt the same about other men as I did about him.

Truth be told, no man has ever made me feel the way that my father did. Not even David. Hulk is the only man who's come close but that's only because he's big like my dad. My father touched me in a way that no other man has been able to figure out.

There must be something wrong with that, though. It can't be right that I've been lusting after my father all these years. I never looked at him again the way I did before he raped me, so why am I starting to feel that way after? I'm in serious need of some counseling.

I can't solve all my problems at once so I put that one on hold. I have party plans to make.

My hit men buddies give me the names of guys in their profession who are also gifted in the kitchen. I want them to prepare a scrumptious meal for all of my special guests.

To further strengthen my position, I hire a bunch of the people from Rasta's to be waiters, hosts and servers. Some work there and some just hang out there. Tony has no idea what he'll be walking into when he enters the hall.

I've told everyone working the party that it's a costume party. They will all wear different costumes to entertain the guests.

For my costume, I've chosen to be a cowgirl. It's not a true cowgirl outfit, though. I've accessorized a Baby Phat catsuit with a pair of lizard cowboy boots and a cowboy hat. I also wear a gun belt sporting Desert Eagle forty-four magnums in both the right and left holsters and a slick leather vest. Of course, underneath it all is my bulletproof vest and a thin body armor for my legs.

The catsuit and boots make my tits and ass look too desirable to ignore. I know what's gonna happen as soon as Big Tony sees me. It'll be difficult waiting for the right moment to spill what I know.

Big Tony arrives fashionably late with the same bodyguards he's been using for years. I can't tell by their expressions if they know anything or if they've been listening to the street talk. I'm not concerned. To say that tonight they are outnumbered is an understatement.

Big Tony starts in on me as soon as he sees me. He lingers too long on my cheeks when he kisses me and once again lets his hands find my butt while he's saying whatever bullshit he's saying.

"You know, Tony, I really wish you'd stop grabbing my ass." I don't try to embarrass him. He and I are the only people who heard what I said. Still, I'm sure he's caught off guard.

"You're all woman, Fatou," he says backing up just enough to get a good look at me. "I loved David, too, but someone has to take care of all of this."

With his fake fucking fat-ass smile, I can't believe he even has the audacity to go there.

"I miss the hell out of David." I lean in close so I can whisper. "But someone's been tightening up my pussy since he's been gone."

I switch away, careful to exaggerate every movement of my luscious body after delivering my first dagger to his heart. By the end of the night, there will be many others.

My motley crew of hit men musicians play a bunch of Italian standards. The mood is festive and everyone seems to be enjoying themselves.

I'm playing the perfect hostess. I walk casually from table to table, from group to group, and hold brief conversations. I'm careful not linger too long at any one place.

My associates from Rasta's are walking around carrying platters of jumbo shrimp with cocktail sauce, caviar on toast points, and bruschetta which is toasted Italian bread topped with chopped tomato, garlic, fresh basil, olive oil and goat cheese.

After another half hour of mingling, I go to the podium and ask everyone to return to their tables. Entrees are to be served as soon as everyone is seated.

There're three entrees from which to choose: capellini coi granchi, lump crabmeat simmered in a creamy white wine sauce served over a bed of angel hair pasta; linguine Portofino, sweet littleneck clams, mussels, shrimp, scallops and fresh garlic simmered in a marinara sauce served over linguine; and pollo ripieno con spinaci, formaggio e pomodoro secci con salsa vino bianco, a filleted chicken breast rolled and stuffed with spinach, cheese and sundried tomatoes and finished with a delicate white wine sauce and a side of shiitake mushrooms sautéed in a garlic butter sauce.

The bar is stocked with wines imported from Italy and an assortment of scotches, whiskeys and rums. It's an alcoholic's paradise.

When everyone has been served, I start the festivities. Big Tony is to be roasted then presented with a plaque.

Friends of Big Tony's come to the podium and give him shit and break his balls with story after story of escapades that Tony experienced in his life and how it affected the person telling about it. Tony has touched a lot of people's lives—some in good ways, others in very bad ways. Tonight, he will pay the piper for all of it.

I go last and start off immediately breaking his balls by saying that no one can grab ass mistakenly on purpose like Big Tony can. Everyone breaks out in laughter, especially the pretty women who have personal knowledge of what I'm speaking about.

I continue to give him shit for another ten minutes before finally saying that some of the stories may not be for everyone.

"So my last story will wait until I get to your table to present you with this plaque. Congratulations, Big Tony!"

There's a wave of applause as I approach him. I give him a hug, and of course he grabs my ass for old time's sake. I can tell that he's really choked up. He's shared a lot of good times and memories tonight.

"So what else do you have to tell me?" he asks after I hand him the giant plaque.

"I've thought about it, and I can't give up any more points on Motherland. David and I busted our asses to get it. It's the only thing I have left that was special and totally exclusive to him and me."

"Is this some type of a joke?"

"No. I'm being serious, Big Tony."

"Well, you need to be something besides serious. I thought you understood the way things worked."

I survey the room and am glad to see that the people from Rasta's are busy attending to Big Tony's table. Some are grating cheese onto the pasta dishes, others grinding fresh pepper. Some are pouring wine, and water glasses are being refilled.

The band members, who are on break at the moment, are holding private conversations with people from Tony's entourage. Even a couple of the chef's come out of the kitchen to receive compliments. I definitely am not on an island by myself. When Ricco comes to my side, it's the last signal that I need.

"I know how things work, Big Tony, but some things are sacred. Otherwise the world would be one big mix of blah without no distinct flavors. It's gonna be my way, and you have to understand."

"No it doesn't!" He starts to get loud. "I remember you when you were nothing."

"The reason I didn't start this conversation at the podium is because I wanted it to be between me and you." I know he hates that I'm suggesting he lower his voice.

"I don't give a shit who hears! I'm the don in this fucking city! Don't you ever forget that."

"I know who you are, Big Tony. And that's why I thought you'd understand how important it is for me to hold my own since I did basically what you did, turn nothing great into something special."

"I don't know shit about that. I've always been special. That's why everyone takes pleasure in making sure that I always get a piece of the pie. No one ever spites Big Tone. Now you're trying to bite the hand that feeds you."

"How are you feeding me, Tony? I've worked my ass off. Haven't I put in long hours like everyone else, Ricco?"

"Don't you say a thing," Tony screams. "Don't you say a fucking word. Haven't I been good to you? Don't try and repay me by standing here with this fucking bitch."

"I thought you were good to me, Papa, but obviously you weren't good enough."

Tony's eyes look like he's just seen a ghost. He's about to shit himself.

"One more thing," I say before drawing one of my guns and putting two bullets between his eyes. "That's Miss Fucking Bitch to you."

CHAPTER EIGHTEEN

Picking Up the Pieces

May 2002

Of course everyone at the party knew what happened, but the same story was repeated over and over to the cops. No one saw shit.

Still, I was smart enough to leave with my people before the cops got there.

It's been a couple days, and I haven't yet spoken to Donny. He must know since his mother was at the party, but I'm not sure if she's talked any sense into him or not by now. Honestly, I don't think she really has to.

Many black men hate their fathers. Donny certainly had more than enough reasons to hate Big Tony. That's why my search ended with the don. Even if Donny had something to do with David's death, I know his father is really the guilty party, not him. Sometimes, you can drive people to do things and act in a certain way even if it's not in their character to do so. Donny needs to heal just like everyone else. So, as far as he's concerned, I decide to forgive and forget.

Following that logic about my own father isn't as easy to do. I am getting counseling but still haven't been able to reach out to him or my mother yet. I could be running out of time, but I can only move as fast as my feelings will allow me to move.

I've also been really caught up in Ricco's case. I can't tell you how many witnesses I have either bribed big time, threatened, or both. At any rate, it doesn't look like the state has much of a case. One by one, their witnesses are disappearing or showing up to recant their previous statements. The results are decent but getting there has been putting a lot of stress on me.

I'm on Long Island, trying to determine my exit strategy when someone rings the bell. Of course I strap up before answering, but I end up not being in any danger. It's only Natali.

Natali wants to talk to me about the escort service. It seems like our bread and butter person is starting to have second thoughts about her work. Not even I can remember the last time she actually serviced a client.

"This has never been my thing, Natali," I tell her. "I got into the because of you. So all I can tell you is the business is not gonna run itself."

"You're right, Fatou. The whole thing was my idea. And it's worked out. But I feel like I've outgrown it."

"I love Redd, too, Natali, but you have to understand that you can't change your entire life over a piece of dick. The life Redd lives is far from a piece of cake whether you know it or not."

"You're trying to tell me this?" she asks sarcastically.

"You're right. I did a lot of things differently after I met David, but I was already damaged goods. I was ready to lash out at anyone and everything. David was just a vehicle for me to release my anger. You, on the other hand, aren't hurting anybody. But you may be hurting yourself when you start talking about leaving your cushy life behind and going out on a limb with Redd."

"That's true," she admits. "But what if I want both of us to leave our respective games?"

"Just because you want Redd to quit doesn't mean that he's going to. Don't you know how many girlfriends, mothers and grandmothers have tried to get their men to leave the game? They're always talking about 'after this or after that'. Remember, if David would've just left everything behind like I asked him to in the beginning he would still be here."

I think I'm getting to her so I approach her and put my arm around her.

"You're my best friend, and I love you, girl. If I didn't, I would've never let you back in here after you disrespected my man's memory and his house. You see, even unstable-ass me can learn to forgive and forget."

"I love you too, girl, and I'm sorry for the things I said. You were in a terrible state, and I just made it worse. I should have put my feelings aside and been there for you."

"You have been there for me. I don't know what I would have done without you."

After much discussion and several hits and misses by the prosecutor's office, the charges against Ricco are eventually dropped. Big Tony's gone and the cops still don't have any leads as to who did it. I feel like this is one of those times where everything is going too good.

I want to nip any surprises in the bud so I decide to have a conversation with Patra. Natali's comments about our bread and butter being disgruntled didn't go unnoticed.

I catch her in the afternoon one day while her kids are napping. I tell Natali not to book her so I can make sure that she has some free time. When I find her, she's laying on one of the beds in the escort service reading The Coldest Winter Ever by Sister Souljah.

I tap on the door frame since the door's already open, and she glances up to acknowledge me. She smiles when she puts the book down, but she has a defeated look on her face.

"Hi, Fatou," she says. "What brings you around here?"

"I was worried about you."

"I'll be OK. I hate to be acting like such a crybaby considering everything you've done for me. I do not want to be the reason for messing up things with your bottom line."

"Is that why you think I'm here?" I ask. "I'm seriously worried about you, Patra."

"I know you have me here doing what I am doing as some type of punishment. I understand that. At least I am able to put myself in a better position to give my kids better opportunities."

"You call this house punishment, Patra?"

"I love the house. I just do not like what I have to do to stay here."

"I have you doing what you do because you're good at what you do. You made more money in the back room than all the other girls who worked at Fifi's combined."

"Yes, but most of the money came from Lama. It was never about me whoring around. It was always about me being in love with him."

"I always wondered if you were really in love with him or just in

170

love with what he gave you."

"He didn't have shit. The man was just as poor as anyone else."

"He wasn't that poor. He never had what I now have, but he wasn't that poor. But I was talking about his ability to give you citizenship in this country. I'm sure you don't want to go back to the motherland."

"Can you blame me? No one wants to go back."

"I don't want to go back either, not anymore. But life has been terrible for me here."

"It seems like you make out OK."

"To a certain extent, I got lucky."

"I wouldn't call it luck," Patra says.

"Then what would you call it?"

"You are a fighter, and fighting is something you have to do when you are a woman in this country. No, if you're in any country. No man or woman is gonna respect you just because you are pretty. You are the type of person who has always earned it."

"I think that I was simply scared and living by instinct. Half the time, I didn't know if I was coming or going."

"But you made the right decisions. I wish I would have thought things out like you did."

"Trust me. I've made my share of mistakes."

"Everyone has. But you have always remained on a very straight path even when you made mistakes. I am curious about one thing, though?"

"What's that?"

"With your brains, why the hell are you doing things like this?"

I look at Patra and analyze her question. I've asked myself the same thing on numerous occasions. Lord knows that Mati has been like an irritating gnat in my ears, asking me shit like this all the time.

"If not this, what else would I do?"

"You could be president of some school or something."

"I can't do that. I don't even have my GED."

"Whose fault is that?"

"It's nobody's fault. It's just that you have to be careful when you're in this country illegally."

"But you have all sorts of connections in City Hall. Surely you can talk to the right people to get the ball rolling."

"Is this about me or you?"

"It's about both of us. Life has been so cruel to us that we found ourselves being arch enemies just because that's what we thought we had to be. But the crabs-in-a-barrel complex is over with. Our lives should be much better than they are. I am not proud looking my children in the face, knowing that I lay on my back with my legs spread all day."

"What else do you know how to do?"

"I do hair, Fatou! Whatever happened to the great big salon you used to say you were gonna open? And what ever happened to all of those clients you used to have?"

I look at her sideways. She isn't supposed to know about any of my plans to open a salon.

"You're not the only one who knows French, Fatou."

"So how come you never said anything?"

"I could not bring myself to do anything underhanded to you after the hospital episode. I just wish that I was strong enough to leave Lama alone, too. I know the situation was painful for you."

"Maybe so, but it was for the best. Your spending so much time with him kept him from breathing down my neck. That gave me all the space and time I needed to grow. I wouldn't be the person I am today if he was on my ass all the time."

"Thank God for small miracles then."

I study Patra and realize that she does indeed have a brain. Like Mati said, never judge a book by its cover.

"So, you wanna do hair and open salons, huh?"

"Who said anything about opening salons? One at a time, girl."

"If you haven't learned anything else about me you should know that I'm not gonna do something unless I plan to do it way big. Making a good first impression is the only way to succeed in business. Never forget that."

CHAPTER NINETEEN

Natural Woman

May-June 2002

After my talk with Patra, I thought about all the hard work I had put into passing the test for my GED. It burns me up that I worked so hard for it and have nothing to show for my efforts.

I decide to call Patrick and vent about it. I also do a lot of cheer-leading, telling him how much I love this country.

Patrick is more concerned with me not losing what I've obtained with fake identification. I have a lot of properties and legal business-es in New York City. Someone's head will roll if the truth ever comes out. Patrick knows his would roll first.

I ask him if he has contacts in Albany or even out of town. Maybe my journey to become a legal citizen can begin somewhere else.

He remembers that he has a contact in Washington. I am immediately excited.

"Yes, Washington. I love D.C.!"

"D.C.? I'm talking about Washington State."

"Washington State? What in the hell is in Washington State?

That's nowhere!"

"But you won't be going there for leisure, Fatou. You'll be going there to handle your business academically. Besides, Seattle is a big party town with plenty of things to do."

"Doesn't it rain a lot in Washington State? You know that the last thing a sister wants to see after getting her hair done up and looking and feeling great is some rain."

"You'll be fine. But I have a question. What will I get after setting all of this up? I've been dying for Patra, you know."

"You're too much, Patrick. But sad to say, I've seen the error of my terrible ways."

"What the hell is that supposed to mean?"

"I can't condone what you're suggesting. If you do it on your own, with whatever gift I give you, fine. I just don't want to be involved in organizing anything traumatic anymore."

"What kind of a gift?"

"You won't be sad. I'll make it worth your while."

"Alright, but this is terrible. Don't you know what type of public service your company has been providing?"

"Well, pretty soon it will be someone else's company. I'm about to wash my hands of everything that makes my heart feel heavy. I'm going in a new direction."

"If you say so."

"Oww, shit! Hold on, Patrick." Suddenly a sharp pain goes through my insides like I've been struck by lightning or something.

"What in the hell is going on over there?" I hear Patrick's voice through the phone. I don't have the energy to respond. As he repeatedly calls my name, his words become more and more faint. In the end, I pass out totally.

When I come to, I'm in a stiff bed with all types of shit in my arm. Natali is holding my hand, sitting in a chair next to the bed.

"Where the fuck am I?" I ask her.

"You're at Saint Luke's Hospital." I look at her real funny. "You know, off Amsterdam."

"I know where the hell it is," I whisper. "But why did you bring me here? You know how nosy these motherfuckers are. I'd rather be in any other hospital than this one."

"Don't worry. Patrick set it up. They won't be asking any questions. Besides, you were in really bad shape. I wanted to get you help as fast as possible."

"Well, I'm glad that you were around. I don't know where all of this came from."

"You're such a liar." Natali gives me the type of look your mother would give you when she's scolding you. "I talked to Mati. She told me that you've been putting off seeing a specialist for a really long time. You're smarter than that, Fatou. You have everything—and too much to lose. But you know the one thing money can't buy you is good health. You have to take care of yourself."

"Yes, Mother."

"This is no joking matter, Fatou. Just wait until the doctor gets in here to talk to you. I'm going out to get a nurse and let her know that you're finally done with your beauty sleep."

Natali walks out. She's trying to be brave for me, but I can tell that something is seriously wrong. I pick up the buzzer and start getting sadistic with it. I want to know what the hell is going on.

An older Caucasian nurse comes into my room looking as if she could be Florence Nightingale. Her movements are methodical. I can tell that she's about her business.

"It seems like someone may need a sedative to relax. All you have to do is buzz us one time, and we'll come. If there was anything seriously wrong the equipment, we would have told you before you ever had the chance to abuse that godforsaken buzzer."

Great, I think to myself. *My nurse is a damned character.*

"It's an emergency," I say. "I want to know what's going on."

"The doctor will be in momentarily," she says. "Just try to relax until he gets here. You don't want to be upsetting yourself."

"That's right," Natali echoes as she returns to the room sipping a cup of tea. "You definitely don't want to upset yourself."

Her look tells me that trouble's on the horizon. Seconds after she enters the room Mati comes in behind her.

"Oh lord," I say. "You didn't have to come here troubling yourself, Mati. I'll be fine."

"Say what you will but I am not waiting to give you your flowers when you're dead. I am going to stay right here until someone with a medical degree tells me that you will be OK."

"Alright, but don't lecture me. My heart is on a pace to heal itself. You don't want to upset the natural progression of things by pushing me off my center. It takes time."

"Well, I brought you a DVD so you can watch a spoken word piece about time. The movie is called *Slam*. It should satisfy your fascination with watching movies."

"You just brought one? I hope I'm not gonna be in here long. I feel bad enough already. I don't need to be watching the news."

"Well, hello there sleepy head." The doctor arrives and interrupts our conversation. "I have a few questions to ask you."

"Good, because I have plenty to ask you," I say.

"Well, me first. My questions deal with correcting your immediate physical health. We can get to your questions later."

"What type of hospital is this? Is everyone gonna give me shit?"

"Fatou!" Mati exclaims, surprised.

"We aim to please," the doctor says.

I learn from the doctor that I have a bleeding ulcer. I've let it go untreated for so long that it's now about the size of a fist. In addition, the excessive bleeding may have damaged one of my kidneys. Tests will need to be run in order to determine where I am on that end, but I was told not to worry too much. A person can function properly with only one kidney.

I know that I'm strong enough to deal with anything, but I don't like how calm Mati and Natali seem. Their personalities are such that they should be freaking out by now.

"Something is wrong here," I say.

"Of course there is," Mati answers snidely. "You are trying to kill yourself off with worry. I will not let it happen."

"I'll learn to relax and take it light, but that's not what I'm talking about. The two of you are too calm. What's going on?"

"Why shouldn't we be calm?" Mati asks. "The doctor says that he will have your ulcer treated in a matter of days. And the kidney situation is all but taken care of. We even have a contingency plan."

"What contingency plan?"

"I'm going to get some breakfast. Rest up child." Mati leaves the room without answering me. I can tell that she has something going on in that diabolical mind of hers.

"What's going on, Natali?"

"We're trying to get you well, OK? And no matter how mad you get in the end, I'm not gonna let you leave me here to battle this crazy world with its crazy people all by myself." Natali has tears in her eyes.

"Now I know something's going on." I stare Natali down since I know I can break her. She isn't as stubborn as Mati.

"You're parents are coming here, OK?" she blurts out. "Your old man is living on borrowed time, but his kidneys are fine. Since he and you have the same rare blood type, he's the perfect candidate to lend you one of his kidneys if it's necessary." ·

"That fucking, Mati!" I say, beyond shocked. "But wait a minute. She couldn't have pulled this off on her own. She doesn't have that type of money. One plan ticket is outrageously expensive from West Africa, so I know what it costs for two. Add to that the visas this country isn't in a hurry to give to people of African descent so she probably needed somebody like Patrick to help her and his help costs a grip. Plus, she doesn't even know any-fucking-body like Patrick. I can't believe you, Natali!"

"OK, I arranged it all. Sue me. All that matters to me is that you'll be OK in the end."

"You send almost every dime you make to your family so you can't afford to bring my parents here either."

"Well, the take from the escort service is a little light."

"You touched my share of the money, didn't you? You know that people have died for a lot less."

"It's a good thing then that you're not in the business of killing anymore, right? So I should be fine."

"I hate you, bitch."

"I love you, too," Natali says.

After hugging Natali for nearly an hour and crying a river of tears, I take a quick nap. When I wake up, Natali—ever the trooper—is asleep in a chair off in the corner.

"Psst," I call out to her. "Yoo hoo!"

She opens her eyes.

"Who the hell is running our business?" I ask.

"You know Suzy's the shit, girl. She works harder than you."

"I guess she's turning tricks, too," I say sarcastically.

"Oh. That business just seems to run itself," she replies.

"Natali, I'm gonna be here for days. You can't be vacationing in here while the world's still going on. It's not gonna slow down to wait for my little ass."

"Be that as it may, I'm not leaving here until the doctor says you're one hundred percent OK."

"With my issues, I'll never be one hundred percent OK. And you know that."

CHAPTER TWENTY

Daddy's Little Girl

June 2002

My ulcer has all but cleared up. But as happy as that makes the doctor, he feels equally bad about my kidneys. One of them can be totally set out to pasture and the other seems to be on life support itself.

I've always tried to be responsible. I can't believe I played around with something as important as my health. I let a simple little ulcer go untreated and now look at my kidneys. I know I don't want to end up like Don Samuels.

Speaking of Don, I got to Big Tony before Big Tony got to him. Of course I let him keep all the money. Honor is a big thing on the streets. I've learned that you can't renege once you've given your word.

Money hasn't cured Don's ills, but it has improved the quality of life in his last days. He's visited me a couple times and tells me how glad he is that I gave him the opportunity to strengthen his relationship with his family before he dies. He says that a father couldn't ask for anything more important than that.

That's the last place I want my mind to go so I try to think of something else. I look over at Natali and she's hunched in her chair, reading a book about a West African Girl in Harlem. It sounds interesting. I'm gonna have to borrow the book from her when she's done.

Mati hasn't been here since early yesterday so I wonder where she's been. But I've had a carousel of visitors—Joe-Joe and Brittany, Ricco, Sarge, Hulk, Redd. But I'm not sure if Redd came for me or for Natali. The bitch thinks that I don't know what they were doing in the bathroom. Whore.

The only person who hasn't visited is Donny. I guess my doing his father in is too much for him to swallow right now. How could he blame me though? He knows how the game is. A life for a life just like in the movie *Next Of Kin* with Patrick Swayze.

I must be psychic because as I'm thinking of Donny, his mother walks in the door.

She's really cute for an older woman. You can tell where Donny gets his looks. They certainly didn't come from Big Tony.

She walks in, and Natali takes her eyes off her book. Natali knows who Donny's mother is and immediately excuses herself.

She comes over to the bed and holds my hand.

"How are you doing, child?" she asks me.

"I'm fine. How are you doing, Miss... I'm sorry, but I never did know Donny's last name."

"It's Ratliff. But don't call me that. You'll make me feel old. Call me Katrina."

"Well, hello Miss Katrina."

"Here we go with the Miss thing again!" she laughs.

"It's not a Miss thing. It's a respect thing."

"Well, I'm not one to argue with someone your age about respect. I wish you just could bottle it up and sell it."

"I don't know why you'd bother. It would just sit on the shelves."

"You're right about that." There's an odd moment of silence. "Listen. I never thanked you for what you did. In one day, you helped strip away decades of shame in my family. We can walk down the street now, holding our heads up high again thanks to you."

"I wish everyone in your family could see things the way you do."

"You're talking about Donny. He's being as difficult as he normally is. But I don't believe he's as upset as people think he is. He's even been hanging out with Ricco."

"I didn't know that."

"Well, he has. I guess the biggest thing that he needs to know is if you're mad at him or not. I think that's why he's been staying away from you."

"I'm not mad at Donny. He's a victim just like the rest of us."

She gives me a look that says she's not certain she believes me. I finally get it.

"And I definitely wouldn't do anything to Donny. If that was the case, it would've already been done."

"Part of me has been thinking that. But Donny keeps saying that he's living and breathing because no one can touch him in the South Bronx."

"Please," I say incredulously. "Donny's my boy, but he does have an ego."

"You're right about that."

"But seriously. I can tell you everything that Donny has done from sunup to sundown everyday since Big Tony left us. But that's not so

I can put my hands on him. It's just, you know, so I can keep on top of things. You can never figure out how people are gonna react when certain things happen. If I didn't want Donny to be here, he wouldn't be here. Period. End of story."

"I'm sure Donny feels the same way."

I don't care about a powerless person trying to show strength. A mother has her pride and should be able to protect her young. Who am I to try to stop her from walking away with her dignity?

"I'm glad we had this talk," I tell her. "Now, can you tell Donny that he'd better get his ass here to see me? My feelings are kinda hurt about him playing me out like this."

"I'm sure it isn't personal. You take care of yourself, OK?"

"I most certainly will."

Miss Katrina Ratliff leaves my room with her head held high. I feel good knowing that I helped put the swagger back in her step.

I'm glad when Natali returns to the room until I notice who she's dragging on her arm. It's Alpha Kone, my father.

I'm sure Binta, my mother, isn't far behind. She's a true African woman and won't come anywhere near me until her husband has test-ed the waters and tells her it's OK.

I give Natali the evil eye before she exits and leaves Alpha with me. But it's too late for her to run interference now anyway. I have to exorcise the demons that have been haunting me for far too long.

Alpha is still a handsome man with a flawless face, but old and defeated now. He's not the pillar of strength I remember him to be. I'm wondering if the same dirty old man curse that swallowed Lama up came to settle the score with him as well.

"How are you, my child?" he asks.

"You'd call me that after what we've shared?" I ask. "I'd think you'd address me by a more familiar pet name."

He ignores me. "How are you feeling?"

"I feel like crap. But I look like I'm doing a lot better than you."

"I know you hate me, and I'm sorry for that. But time does heal all wounds," he says.

"Well, time has not diminished the thoughts I've had about you. I'm probably the only girl in the world who every night dreams about making love to her own father. Do you think that that's OK, Alpha?"

"Allah's mercy and wisdom will prevail in all things. So will his justice. If I am to be punished for what I've done, I will be. I only seek your forgiveness. And I hope to give you more than I have taken away. I love you, my princess, and I'm proud of the woman you've become."

With that, he backs out of the room, too ashamed to even hug his own daughter. I feel like I'll never get the chance to have those strong arms wrapped around me again.

Right on cue, Hulk walks in the door ranting and raving.

"I may have to cut off things with you," he says.

"Nigga, you ain't got shit to cut off. Well, maybe I can cut up that shriveled up little…"

"Anyway," he says, interrupting me. "Watch your mouth. There's a pretty little lady outside your door. I swear she's the only person I've ever met who's cuter than you."

I start to get really excited. As mad as I want to be at my mother, I'll always love her. It's been such a long time and I'm reeling inside. I'm anxious to see her face.

She comes into my room and runs to me, screaming and crying. Her hysterical behavior makes me get hysterical right along with her. Hulk quietly leaves us alone.

We hug each other tightly and rock back and forth. It's the kind of homecoming greeting any child and parent would want. The thing is, though, that I haven't come home except inside of me. Home is where my heart is right now—in total, one hundred percent synch with my mother.

We talk and talk about the village. She tells me who's still living, who's passed, who's become an elder, who's gotten married. I feel like I never left.

Then she asks me lots of questions. She wants to know how I'm supporting myself. I give her an abbreviated, not totally factual version of how I don't have a care in the world money-wise.

Next, she wants to know if my heart belongs to anyone. I tell her that it used to, and I think she misunderstands me.

"Yes, it was tragic finding out how Alpha was tricked all of these years. And to think that because of a lie, Lama has a litter of children by his own sister."

"Mama, what are you talking about?"

"You don't know? I thought you said that you used to be madly in love with someone."

"Yes, but not Lama. Of course I learned to love him. But he never truly had my heart. Yet, what's this about Lama and his sister having children?"

"Oh my God. Maybe I've said too much. It may be better if we just let the past stay in the past and continue the healing process."

"No, Mom. You have to tell me what you're talking about."

"Are you sure, child? You're already in the hospital."

"I'm positive."

"Well, an elder telephoned Lama when he found out that his parents had secretly shipped their daughter to America so they wouldn't have to honor the agreement to have the first daughter in our families marry a son. The deception nullified our agreement. We didn't even have to repay the dowry. Lama hung up the phone on the elder and stopped answering his calls. His sister has been here all along without Lama knowing they were related. Yet, Lama was so evil that I doubt the knowledge would have stopped him from sleeping with Patra."

"Wait. Patra? Patra is Lama's sister?"

"You know her? You've seen her?"

"Yes. She stays at my house and works for me. Oh my God. She's gonna go crazy when she hears this."

"Are her babies healthy?"

"Yes, they are well."

"Fatou, maybe telling her is not the best thing to do," my mother says, looking worried. I understand where she's coming from.

Why should we poison Patra, and possibly even her children, with knowledge that won't do them any good whatsoever? But, if we keep it from her, she'll never be able to return to our homeland.

"I can't believe this," I say. "Patra and Lama are brother and sister and had all of those children together...So how long was it before you knew that they were brother and sister?"

"It wasn't long at all. Alpha was incensed. He went to an elder and had your marriage nullified. Lama refused to listen to reason. Rather than give you up, he turned his back on everyone."

"So I could have been free a long time ago? I could have even come back home?"

"There is nothing left there for you, my child. We sent you here so that you could blossom. You haven't disappointed us. In fact, you've made us very, very proud."

I feel like a smacked ass. My mother is sitting here, praising me, and I've done everything under the sun. I've killed, sold drugs, prostituted women—I've been a total menace to society.

Out of nowhere, my tears return. These fresh tears, however, aren't the happy tears I cried when I first saw my mother. These tears are for all the horrible things I've done. These tears are for all of the miles I've strayed from my heritage and upbringing. I'm an embarrassment to my village. I'm an embarrassment to Mother Africa. I'm an embarrassment to myself.

My mother hugs me and tries to console me. It's not an easy task. Every single shady deed I've done resurfaces in my mind.

"My child... I spoke at length with Alpha the day you hung up the phone on me..."

"Forget about it, Mom."

"No. I will not forget about it. I will never forget about it. And I will never forgive myself."

"But you didn't know."

"You are correct. I did not know. But a woman should never give so much of her own power over to a man that she would allow even the thought of something so terrible to happen. Alpha took away many years from your childhood, and if it's the last thing I do in this world—if it's the last thing that he does in this world—you're going to get every last one of those years back."

"I love you, Mom."

"I love you too, my child. And your father loves you. That's why with the limited time he has left to live, he's going to use it to make sure that you are healthy again."

"What can he give me? I already have everything. I just need time, Mom. That's all. I just need more time."

"And you are going to get it. To answer your question, the one thing that your father can give you is a kidney."

"But isn't he too sick? An operation like that might kill him."

"And if it does, you can have both his kidneys."

I finally comprehend what my mother and father have been saying.

"Alpha understands what it means, and he fully accepts his responsibility. Now you must accept it."

"I don't know, Mom. It seems so...merciless."

"You're father will be very offended if you do not go along with his plan. After doing what he did to you, he feels that this is the least he can do."

"As bad as it was, Alpha's actions motivated me. I'm still here, Mom. It didn't kill me. It only made me stronger."

"Your father is meeting right now with your doctor. I imagine that they are testing his blood and the strength of his kidneys. He will have the operation to give you one of his kidneys right away. Hopefully, everything will work out. But if it does not, you will be in this hospital for another week before they can give you his other kidney."

It's eerie listening to my mother talking about my father having an operation he knows will most likely kill him. I wonder if the idea was his or hers. It doesn't matter, though. No matter whose idea it was, I'd be sadistic to go along with it. They must be out of their minds.

"Mom, what makes you think that I'd agree to this?"

"Because you have to. You don't have any other choice."

"I could just get up and walk out of this hospital."

"You'd never make it to the front door. I'd wrestle you down to the ground like a goat and beat you with a strap if I had to."

Wow. My mother is talking about whipping my ass. Amazing.

"What would you do without Alpha?"

"I would manage. Maybe I would try to be a comfort to as many people as I possibly could in our homeland. America is too fast for me. I have only been here a few hours, but it has been a few hours too long. As soon as I know that you are well, I will be leaving."

"I am OK, Mama. And I can't think of anything happening that would make me not be OK. If you hate it here so much, you shouldn't stay."

"I just arrived, and you are trying to shoo me away already!" she cracks.

"It's not that, Mom. It's just...you don't have to witness...I mean, you don't have to go through the pain you're about to go through."

"I have been with your father for as long as I can remember, and I am not leaving here without him. Even if I have to take him home in a wooden box."

"You really love him, don't you?"

"More than you will ever know. And I do not just love him. I forgive him. It was a cruel, cruel thing he did to you. But you are so beautiful. How could I blame him? I am just glad you turned out OK."

I can't say that I appreciate all of what my mother has said, but I'm sure she's as caught up in the awkwardness of the moment as I am.

I find myself getting sleepy again so I beckon for her to sit on my bed and cuddle with me. It feels just like I remember. It's the last thing I remember before I fall asleep.

CHAPTER TWENTY-ONE

Healing

July 2002

It's been a few weeks since my mother left me full of life, and my father traded his for mine.

I didn't send her off empty-handed. I gave her resources totaling over one hundred million dollars with one simple instruction— rebuild our homeland and help as many of our people as possible.

I'm sure my mother will become an overnight celebrity when she returns. But she doesn't care about stuff like that. She's a legitimate sweetheart who really has a bleeding heart.

I introduced Mom to Patra and her children before she left. And of course I let her meet Mati. She fell in love with her right away, especially after I told her that Mati was the only person who cared for me when I first arrived.

They spent an afternoon walking around Central Park with Frankie and Jimmy looking after them. I'm sure my mother wondered what that was about, but I let her wonder. I am not about to let anyone try to kidnap her.

Mati tells me that she loves what I've done for Patra. She says I am heavenly to forgive her in spite the terrible things she did to me.

I haven't yet told Mati about the salons. I'm opening a bunch of them, and Patra will run them for me. I won't be totally isolated from the daily operations, but I have other things to do. Still, I figure that I'll spend about twenty to twenty-five hours a week in one of the shops just to make sure my skills don't suffer.

I've met with a couple young brothers named Crim and C-Style who own a production company called Up and Coming Productions / Manifest Entertainment. They're helping me develop and shoot commercials that will be aired on Time Warner and Cablevision.

Patrick has hooked Patra and me up with a school in Seattle so we can get our G.E.D.'s. Afterward, when we return to New York, we will be part of a ceremony to become naturalized citizens. Natali will be joining us in the ceremony.

We'll be taking classes at City College, too. Even if we are busy with other things, we will get our Bachelor's Degrees no matter how long it takes. I can't have idiots running any of my companies, whether it's me or her.

Natali has a year left before she receives her Bachelor's Degree, and I've already paid her tuition. I surprised her last week when I told her that I have also paid her full tuition to Syracuse University Law School.

My plan is for Natali to run a company that assists foreigners with becoming naturalized citizens in America. In my opinion, when your skin is dark, the government gives you too much shit. Natali is forever running her mouth and jumping in other people's business so she'll do fine.

193

I get Patrick to help me start a non-profit organization that helps women who have been raped by a family member or friend to get over the harsh psychological wounds. Mati bubbled with excitement when I told her about it. I've already hired a publicist from Brooklyn named Staci Shands to handle all the promotions, and I think we're scheduled to be on Oprah pretty soon and the doors haven't even opened yet.

Hulk is picking me up from the hospital so that he can take me to Rasta's so I can tie up the final loose ends with my involvement in the game. I just spoke to my doctor about my kidneys, and the prognosis is excellent.

Rasta's is full of life when we arrive. Beenie Man is pumping from the jukebox and a couple of young girls are winding their bodies to the sounds.

I know that they aren't legal yet so it disgusts me how some of the older men are lusting over them. I'm gonna have my hands full with my foundation.

I turn my attention away from the young girls and see the fellas sitting in my favorite corner. I walk over and greet them all with hugs, even Donny.

I'm glad he came to visit me at the hospital. We had a long talk and it was very enlightening.

Donny told me that he had been bitching to Big Tony about David promoting Ricco, but he didn't wish Ricco or David any harm. He just couldn't understand why Ricco always got treated like royalty when he was really Big Tony's son not him. Donny didn't know at that point that Ricco was his brother. I guess I just didn't ask the right questions of Donny when he was pumped full of truth serum.

Big Tony adored David as a businessman. And he didn't have a problem with Ricco either. But his conscience started to bother him about treating Donny so badly over the years. He promised Donny that he'd set up a meeting between him and David so that he could straighten things out.

Donny says that Big Tony was tripping at the meeting. He was very disrespectful towards David and kept saying inappropriate things about me and my body parts. I don't know what Big Tony expected David to say when he said shit like "her ass is so plump and luscious and her titties are heavenly" but he kept repeating dumb shit like that over and over.

David finally had enough and prepared to leave. He told Big Tony that he'd take his feelings under consideration and let him know what time it was. He left to go meet with Ricco. Big Tony wasn't too far behind him. That was the last time Donny said he saw David alive.

To think, all of the drama wasn't about Donny or Ricco. It was just about a dirty old Italian man wanting some young black African pussy.

When we all sit down, I order a round of drinks. I had called ahead to make sure they had champagne. The waitress brings us our drinks along with the champagne, flutes and maraschino cherries.

I let everyone know that it's OK to sip on their drinks, but they have to wait until after the meeting to pop the champagne. I let it sit chilling on the corner table.

"OK, gentlemen," I say. "Let me get straight to the point."

They brace themselves like I'm about to give them the secrets to the fountain of youth.

"I've spoken to Julius of the Bosco family, and he doesn't have any problem with Donny and Ricco running things together here in the states for me. In fact, he'll be coming to America shortly to bring honor back to his family's name." Everyone gives Donny and Ricco pounds and other congratulations.

"If the two of them decide to tell you why I made my decision, it's up to them. But that's not all. Sarge and Rottweiler are also promoted to captains since we want you to spread out as far into Jersey as you wish. Joe-Joe, you'll be a captain, too, on one condition."

"Just tell me what I have to do," he says.

"You have to branch out into Syracuse and Connecticut. You can take as many workers as you want. But remember that you have to promote someone to lieutenant who can hold down Brooklyn the same way you can. If you have to visit from time to time and crack some heads, I'm sure everyone will understand."

"No doubt," Joe-Joe responds.

"Redd is officially out of the business," I continue.

"What?" Redd's outburst lets me know that I've surprised him.

"You can't be engaged to my best friend and keep doing this shit. She's about to be running one of my legit businesses." He looks heated. "Just hold off on your comments until I'm finished," I say.

I take a deep breath and continue, getting choked up in the process.

"You've all been very loyal to me as you were all loyal to David. As a reward for your service, I'm gonna hit you all off with a little sumthin sumthin."

I hand all of them an envelope.

"You'll find a key and instructions on where to go pick up your rewards. Don't ask me and don't tell anyone what little bonus I leave you with. If it were up to me, though, I'd take the bonus and tell Julius to kiss my ass. I'd get out of this crazy-ass game for good. But you are all grown-ass men, and you're gonna do whatever you feel your big and bad enough to do."

"I didn't forget you, Hulk. I've set everything up so you can buy a bunch of taxis from Motherland's fleet. You can name the company whatever you want but the idea is that within the next month or so, no Motherland taxi will be involved in illegal activities. I'm sure Donny will school you on everything."

"No doubt," Donny says.

"Just like with them, Hulk, I'm setting you up with a business so you can use your own judgment as to whether or not to keep balling or to go legit. All that I can say is that I left it up to you since I couldn't figure out if I was gonna give you any more of this pussy or not."

All the fellas laugh. Hulk looks embarrassed that I let the cat out of the bag.

"I can say this, though," I continue. "I won't be giving my shit up anymore to anybody involved in the game. That shit is dead to me now. As crazy as I was, I'm surprised that I've lived this long in this game."

"Fatou, you's a crazy-ass alright!" Joe-Joe says laughing.

"I did what I had to do. Now I don't have to do it anymore." I get up, all teary-eyed again. "I'll miss you, fellas. Don't call me with no dirty ass phones but stay in touch. Maybe you'll come check me out when I give a speech or something at one event or another."

I turn and walk away before I start crying. I'm gonna miss the guys. They helped a scared little girl become a woman.

I'm sure they'll all be glad to know that I left them a key to one of the properties I bought specifically for this purpose. When they go into the house, they'll know where to look—the same hiding place we would use in any other circumstance.

I left them all ten million dollars a piece. They can buy a lot of doughnuts with that kind of money so I hope they don't keep trying to make it and put themselves further at risk.

But I can't live for them or make their decisions. Like I said, they're grown-ass men.

For me, there's a wicked, wicked world out there that I plan to make a big difference in.

EPILOGUE

August 2002

I walk into the foundation wearing a Vera Want pantsuit and Prada shoes. My sunglasses are Prada as well. For a really casual and conservative look, I'm dressed to a tee.

I've decided to meet with the troubled teenage girls I'll be helping this year a week early. Most of them are from boroughs in New York. But one hard case, Jennifer Wiley, is from Baltimore, Maryland. Her mother recognized me when I went on a short trip to the harbor and begged me to let her daughter be in my program. She must've seen me on Oprah.

To be in the program, parents of the students must agree to allow me to mend them by any means necessary. Some of them will need counseling, some of them will need to be on birth control so they don't make any further mistakes with their lives, and some of them need the wet ass and switch treatment. Whatever I decide, they can't bitch about it. Unless I abuse them. But then I'm not dumb enough to do anything stupid like that.

As I approach the door, I hear them wilding out. I take a deep breath and enter the room and most of them chill. I scratch my nails across the blackboard so everyone else can come on board the respect train. All but one girl pays attention—Jennifer Wiley.

"I don't know if you all realize this," I start my introduction ignoring Jennifer. "But most of you have a problem. If you didn't have a problem, you wouldn't be here.

"Anyway, whatever you thought your problem was before you got here is nothing. I'm the only problem you'll have from now on. If you can survive me, you'll be just fine."

Jennifer is still acting up, and I've had just about enough of her.

"You don't think, shit, eat, sleep or breathe unless I tell you to. And I'd hate to find out what would happen to one of you if you bled without telling me that it's that time of the month.

"Your world begins and ends with me. Like the cash money brothers in the movie *New Jack City*, I'm all you've got."

"Who the fuck is this bitch?" Jennifer Wiley snaps out loud.

All of the other girls give a collective, "Ooooooooooh." They know my work. Jennifer, though, has made her first big mistake.

I calmly stroll over to her after placing my pointer down on the desk. I don't look too eager, and I definitely don't look shocked. I'm sure this first battle of wills or test or whatever these young bitches want to call it will be like taking candy from a baby.

"What did you say?" I ask.

"I asked who are you," she spits back snidely.

"That's not exactly what you said. I think it was more like, 'who the fuck is this bitch.'"

"So what. Same shit."

I reach back as far as I can and steal the fuck out of her. She's lucky she's not related to me or I wouldn't have had an open hand.

I pull her up off the floor by the neck of her shirt and say, "That's Miss Bitch to you" then I fling her back down in the chair.

"Does anyone else have anything they need to get off their chest?" There's complete silence.

"I don't know who in the hell you think you're fucking with, but if you think I'm some soft-ass bitch you're gonna run over, you must be out of your rabbit-ass minds. Whatever's in your head, wherever you want to go, I've been there and done that. You can act tough if you want, but just like tough-ass Jennifer over there, you'll be picking yourself up off the floor."

I walk over to Jennifer's desk and stand in front of her.

"You're first assignment is a two page, single-spaced paper on me. You're to tell me who I am and where I come from. The lesson here, class, the lesson here, Jennifer, is that you better know who in the hell you're dealing with before you start popping off at the mouth. If you fuck with the wrong person, you may end up six feet under, Jennifer."

She doesn't answer me so I get right up in her face and yell.

"Jennifer!"

"Yes," she whispers like a scared-ass little baby.

"Just so you know, if you would've spoken to me like that six months ago, I would've beaten the shit out of you or put a bullet in your brain. Do you understand?"

"Yes," she whispers.

"Do you understand?" I'm screaming loudly in her face.

"Yes," she says loud enough for everyone to here.

I relent and walk back to the front of the class.

"No one in here has been through what I've been through and I hope that no one ever will. But with your help, that statement won't just be words. I'm gonna tell you the total truth of my life story. I won't hold anything back. Then, if you let me, I'll help you get rid of some of the pain that you're in so you can become productive, successful black women. There's nothing more powerful than that.

"Now, let's get started."

The Lesbian's Wife

A new novel by

Sidi

PROLOGUE

I'm staring at Sharyn in disbelief, not knowing why she wants me to rehash every little horrific detail regarding my life over the past four years. The pain that I endured makes me want to scratch someone's eyeballs out. And since Sharyn is the person behind all my tears right now, I'm thinking that it might be hers.

"It's best if you just let it out, Aicha," she says.

"No, it's Nikki. Don't ever call me Aicha again. I mean it, Sharyn! Don't ever call me Aicha."

My entire body is shaking and tears are streaming down both my cheeks and neck. I'm furious at Sharyn for taking me back to a place I never want to go again. But I can't be too mad at her, though. If it weren't for her, I'd still be captive. My life would still be a living hell.

Maybe I shouldn't have gone through life half asleep. Maybe if I would've paid attention to what was going on around me, I wouldn't have ended up a victim. Maybe I could have done something differently. I say that, but I know that there really wasn't anything that could've been done differently, and if Sharyn hasn't done anything else, she's convinced me that I am not to blame for the tragedy I suffered at the hands of a crazy man.

"He's the one who was wrong, Nikki," Sharyn says right on cue. "He's the monster, and you were the innocent victim."

Fuck that, I think to myself.

I hate the fact that I was a victim. I know that I never wanted to be. Yet, as much as I want to say that I'll never be a victim again, I'm sure that I can't say it. In life there are no guarantees. I'd loved to say that I'd die before I'd be a victim again. But when I was a victim, I was too afraid to put myself out of my misery. To the contrary, I endured every little bit of the torture. And that's what scares me the most, knowing that I didn't take extreme measures to end my suffering, and if I ever again had to face a nightmare like the one I just escaped, I don't know if I could.

I rarely sleep through the night anymore. I always wake up shaking, sweating and terrified. I'm convinced that I'm on Africa's Ivory Coast instead of being safe and sound in America.

The funny thing is that I was so in a hurry to go to Africa. Who wouldn't be? Africa is the cradle of all civilization. I'd advise everyone to visit the motherland at least once in their lifetime if they have the chance. Well, at least I would have advised them of such in the past, but now I'm not so sure. I think if it's a woman, I'd tell her that she'd better be careful. I wouldn't want what happened to me to happen to her. I don't think that I'd wish that on my worse enemy.

If a woman doesn't have a pack of girlfriends to go with her, I'd tell her to travel as much as she wants as long as it's in America. There are hunters out there in foreign countries, and believe it or not, young, attractive women are the prey. And if you're foreign to that country, you have very few resources to depend on for help. You're pretty much out on your own and forced to depend on yourself for survival. Some make it and some don't. Just as mentally, some overcome the tragedy and some don't. The cruelties they suffered at the hands of the abusive male scum of the earth defines the rest of their lives and they're unable to function. They're lost within their abduction and no one knows if they'll ever be found.

That's why I really do hope that all women take me seriously. Yes, I'm trying to get my own head together, but when I do, I plan to speak to women about the perils they will face out there in foreign lands. And if I save one life—if I prevent one woman from going through what I went through—all the tears that I'll cry while rehashing my own horrible story will be worth it.

Take heed of my story. Pay very close attention to the mistakes I made. No, pay close attention to everything I did, especially the things that any normal young girl would have done. Because you never know who's going to sell you down the river. You never know who's going to turn his back on you and put you in a position where you're lost and lonely in a foreign land with no one to turn to. All you'll know is that you're abducted and at the whim of whomever stole you away.

So listen up ladies because it could be you. It could happen to you.

Mandingo
The Golden Boy

Coming soon...
another new novel by

Sidi

PROLOGUE

Denise Jackson

January 2003

Although I'd been with boys before in high school, that's just what they were—boys. And none of them had the length and girth of the grown-ass man standing in front of me. I swear to God, he has to be longer than a ruler and wide enough to fuck up some of my internal shit. Still, I have to go through with this. That's the only way I'm gonna know if he'll be to women what I am to men—the best damned sex money can buy.

I'm scared to ask him to continue taking his clothes off. The bulge in his boxers is very impressive, and I'm afraid his dick is gonna spring out and knock me into the wall or something. To allay my fears, I try to concentrate on a different part by turning my attention to the rest of his body.

The muscles ripping out of his chest and arms make him look like a Mr. Universe contestant. Yet he's not so diesel that it's a turn-off. His six-pack stomach and his thighs are so lean and developed he could race against a horse. He's a strong stallion, alright. The stud-muffin every woman dreams about but never has the chance to experience. I'm about to audition him to make sure he's capable of making their wildest dreams come true. Well, at least those women who can afford him.

"Do you want me to take these off?" he asks in a heavily accented voice.

I feel the lump in my throat grow larger.

"Sure, sweetie," I answer as calmly as I can. "Where'd you say you were from? Africa?" I ask him even though I already know the answer.

"I am from the Mandingo tribe," he replies proudly.

"Nigga, you ain't never lied!"

As he pulls his boxers down, I see it's going to be worse than I thought. He's got a good twelve inches and he's only half hard.

Goddamn! I say to myself. *Some serious fucking is about to go down.*

CHAPTER ONE

Mandingo

As Denise steps out of her dress revealing a silky Victoria's Secret chemise, all of my problems become irrelevant. All that matters to me are the ample breasts straining to stay inside her negligee. Her thighs are thicker than those of any of the pale faces that walk the halls of Columbia University and her butt is a sight for sore eyes. I look up into the air and thank Allah for also giving Denise the brains to make it into one of the toughest schools in America.

I've been lusting after Denise since she befriended me a year ago when I first arrived here. I guess the connection that blacks in America have with each other kicked in when she saw me. Back then, she didn't know I was African. I guess all she cared about was that I was one of the few dark faces in the lily-white crowd. I didn't care what the reason was, though. All that mattered to me was that she was the prettiest woman I'd ever seen in my life and she was talking to me. Just a few words and I was making plans for our wedding and honeymoon, especially our honeymoon.

Regrettably for me, I learned that there were a few problems with the plans I was making for Denise . First and foremost, she is what Americans call a carpet-muncher, meaning that she is attracted to other women. That difficulty alone loomed largely enough but, additionally, her occupation was another disqualifying factor. To put it bluntly, she was a high priced call girl, and I was a broke college student. We were definitely not a match made in heaven.

Even though Denise and I became close, I always beat her upside her head with questions about why with all that she had going for herself would she still decide to degrade herself by selling her body. She'd always say, "You're my boy but your broke-ass is just like all those other niggas trying to get some pussy for free." She had a point, but I still wasn't wrong. There are a million things a woman can do besides prostituting herself. All it takes is a little hard work.

Damn. Now I feel like a hypocrite. I'm talking all of that trash about Denise but the only reason she's about to give me some is because she wants to make sure I'll please the rich clients she has lined up for me. But hell, any excuse to be with this bombshell is good enough for me. She has a body like Vivica Fox and a face like Stacey Dash. Allah forgive me for the illicit acts

I'm about to commit but I don't know a man who's strong enough to withstand her charms. I'm so glad Karen Steinberg told her about our little run-in.

Karen was a country girl from Kentucky who put the C, O, U, N, T, R, and Y in the word. I swear if you look in Webster's you'll see a picture of her smiling face right next to country. But I ain't mad at her though.

For one, she's one of the smartest people to ever graduate from high school in her state. How else do you think she got here? Poor white trash can't afford this place just like we can't.

The other reason I ain't mad at her is she looks like a blond-haired, blue-eyed Daisy Duke. Keep it real, your eyes are glued to the TV, too, whenever you can catch the Dukes of Hazard reruns on Spike TV. What man wouldn't be lusting after Daisy Duke? Not to say that I was lusting after Karen Steinberg, but I noticed her.

Karen Steinberg has breasts similar to Denise 's and long, flowing legs. She's pretty much the classic white bombshell. Kinda tall and slim with big titties. She does have a little phatty for a white girl. Yet, still, like I said, I wasn't all big on her. She stepped to me.

I was in the cafeteria one day when she came in. A couple of the resident loudmouths started talking trash to her after she grabbed her food so I motioned for her to sit with me. I guess I just felt bad for her. And I knew that the only reason they were clowning with her in the first place was because she wouldn't sleep with any of them. Nevertheless, I was certain that they would calm that shit down once she sat with me and I wasn't wrong. Soon as Karen Steinberg's ass hit the chair all of her hecklers became mute church mice. The resulting silence gave us the perfect opportunity to hold our own little private conversation.

Karen wanted to know what it was like in Africa. She asked if we still ran around hunting bears with spears. Although I thought that was an ignorant, racist question, I also found it amusing that those myths still exist.

I didn't answer her, Instead, I asked her if she still wrestled the pigs in the slop pen. She started laughing. I guess she got my point because she changed the subject.

She asked me why blacks got mad about some myths and were quick to cling to others. Of course I didn't know what she meant so I asked her to be more specific. Her response made me fall out.

She said, "You got mad about me asking you if you were a hunter but if I asked you if you had a big, African dick you would have been quick to agree with me."

After I finished laughing, I said, "That's because your first assumption was ridiculous but your second is true."

"Yeah, right," she said. "Everyone knows that the myth about black guys being bigger than white guys. It's legend."

"Nah, baby girl, it's an actual fact," I said proudly.

"Well, show me," she replied.

"What? You can't be serious."

"I'm dead serious," she said, unaware that that was the beginning of the end for her.

We went back to my dorm room and I put on some reggae. I thought Shabba Ranks was appropriate for the moment.

I started gyrating my body to the rhythms of Shabba as I undressed. I could tell that she was more than impressed with my body. After watching her stare at my chest and arms, I decided to rub some baby oil on them to make them glisten. I planned to intensify whatever pleasure this naive white girl was feeling as she lusted over my African features. And, truth be told, she had know idea what the fact of my being of the Mandingo tribe meant. She was definitely about to find out.

When I finally got down to taking off my boxers she gasped. "Is that thing real?" she asked.

I grabbed her arm and led her to me.

"Come on over here, girl, and find out."

She started stroking my dick while she kissed my neck. I could feel myself starting to elongate. Soon I would be at my full fifteen inches.

I smiled when her kisses went from my chest to my stomach. She looked in amazement at my python and muttered repeatedly, "Oh my God."

"Don't pray to Jah now, baby girl," I said. "Your mouth got you into all of this trouble you're in."

I got tired of playing with Karen Steinberg so I finally grabbed the top of her shoulders and guided her down to her knees.

"So, what are you going to do with this big African dick?" I asked her. Without responding, she showed me.

Believe me when I tell you, the myth about white girls knowing how to suck a golf ball through a straw is not a lie. Come to think of it, a redneck, country-ass white girl has even more skills than a regular one. I didn't know that then, but I do now. But I'll tell you about that later. Let me get back to Karen Steinberg and her talented mouth.

At first, she kissed the tip. It was like a series of quick pecks on the lips. But instead of it being my lips, it was the round, sensitive head of my dick.

Out of nowhere, she glanced up at me with the most devilish grin I've ever seen then she took the plunge. She skillfully took me inside her mouth and wrapped her lips around my dick as if she was giving it a bear hug. All the while, she stared deeply into my eyes.

There's something about a woman looking in your eyes while

she's pleasuring you orally. It's a reassurance that lets you know that she knows exactly what she's doing and who she's doing it to. And she was doing it to death.

She bobbed her head up and down as her mouth made slurping sounds each time she swished her tongue.

"Suck that big, African dick!" I demanded, encouraging her.

I doubt that she needed my encouragement, though. She was already going to town.

When her oral prowess started to feel too good, I wanted her to stop. I wasn't going to let her get away with just a Lewinsky. I wanted to pound her white pussy for all it was worth, especially because of the dumb shit she said to me earlier.

"Are you ready for me to ruin that white hole?" I asked.

She started shaking her head and mumbling through slurps on my dick. Yet, that wasn't enough for me. I wanted to hear her speak in plain English.

I pulled my dick out of her mouth roughly and started smacking her in the face with it.

"Beat me with that black dick, Mandingo," she said while catching her breath. "Beat me with it."

I had never understood why my uncle Moriba cheated on his wives even though he had three of them and therefore shouldn't have been bored with any of them. But as I was severely degrading and disrespecting Karen Steinberg, the reasons started to become clear to me.

I would never be seriously involved with Karen Steinberg. But she's a master at sucking dick so I wouldn't mind letting her do it to me again. I just didn't want her to feel like I thought she was special.

She had given me some oral sex that made me go berserk. And I was about to get some white pussy for the first time. I didn't care about Karen Steinberg so told myself I could do whatever I wanted with her wothout explaining myself. She really didn't fucking matter to me then. So I fucked the shit out of her that day.

Karen Steinberg was every man's fantasy—a piece of ass you could do whatever the hell you wanted with none of the bitching and moaning you usually had to deal with. She was the perfect "other woman" to me. She could have been any of the women my uncle Moriba cheated on his wife with. But that day, she was my first victim at Columbia.

After smacking her repeatedly in the face with my dick, I was finally ready to fuck her.

"Turn around," I yelled at her.

"You're too big for that way," she said with pleading eyes.

"I'm just a man about to prove that certain myths are not myths. Just turn the fuck around and take what I'm about to give to you."

Karen Steinberg remained on her knees while she turned

around slowly…cautiously…deliberately.

I paused to stare briefly, somewhat in awe at how nice her ass was for a white girl, round and plump. It definitely wasn't a wide, board butt like other white chicks. It poked out just the way I like it.

After putting on my Magnum condom, I nudged forward to tease her with the tip for a moment. She rocked back eagerly. I knew that wouldn't last for long though. Her ass was about to run for the hills when I really started giving her the dick.

For fifteen minutes, I gave it to her an inch at a time. As every minute passed, I gave her another inch. By the time it reached ten minutes, she was ready to pass out. I was having none of that, though. I smacked her ass really hard until it turned red. I giggled to myself, pleased at how it wiggled like jelly. She looked back at me speechless. I could tell that she wanted to holler or scream or moan or at least tell me to stop smacking her ass so hard. My dick must have been killing her. Her breaths were caught somewhere in her throat. She wasn't able to make the minutest of sounds.

After I had made her take all of me, I started growing bored with the silence. I decided it was time to make Karen Steinberg get a sore throat.

I braced myself carefully behind her and grabbed her small waist tightly with both hands. I rammed myself into her as hard as I could. With each thrust I got more turned on by the way her ass was jiggling. Not to mention her whimpering had me really feeling myself. But it was still not enough.

I rocked back enough to totally remove myself from her then thrust myself back in. She let out a loud shriek.

At that point, I knew I had her where I wanted her so I started repeating the process of taking my dick out and thrusting it back in.

"Oh shit, Mandingo! Goddamn. Oh my damn. Fuck!"

Karen Steinberg was shouting out combinations of curse words I'd never heard before.

Yeah I thought. I was wearing her ass out.

I had no idea about Karen Steinberg's previous sex partners. But I will say that she had one of the tightest pussies I ever had. At the time, I thought that she was so tight because white men have little dicks. My experiences with other white girls after Karen Steinberg clued me in that it wasn't true. It was just her. With that little-ass pussy, I must have been killing her.

I rammed my dick in and out of Karen Steinberg for about ten minutes until her shit started to get to me. Then I put the whole thing inside of her and started grinding it as deep as I could. If I remember correctly, I think I felt my dick hit her kneecap. I don't fucking know how and I know I didn't care. All that mattered to me at the time was that she had some good-ass pussy.

I can't even say that her shit was good for a white girl. She could have been red, black, green or orange, it didn't matter. Her shit was popping. It may have been the best shot in my life. That's why I kept fucking her even after that night. And I'm glad she wanted more. I thought it would just be one and done after I degraded her the way I did.

When I felt myself getting ready to come, I pulled out of Karen Steinberg and pulled the rubber off. She sighed as if she felt instant relief then I started smacking her in the face with my dick again. Eventually, I shoved it in her mouth and started barking out commands.

"Suck this big, black dick you white whore," I yelled at her. "Suck it," I repeated over and over as she obliged me.

After a couple of slurps from her talented mouth, I think I shot a gallon of come into her mouth while holding the back of her head to ensure that she didn't move. Once the last drop came out, I relaxed and slumped backwards.

She started gagging like a five hundred pound man was choking her with both hands. Then she ran to the sink and continued to gag while simultaneously spitting into the sink. Finally, she stomped over to me and preceded to tear me a new asshole.

"You have some fucking big-ass balls, you freakin' African," she screamed. "Some big-ass balls."

"What the fuck is wrong with you?" I asked, pretending to be totally oblivious to her issue.

"You fucking come in my mouth? That's what you do? You fucking come in my mouth?"

"What do you mean?" I said. "If you weren't cool with it, why the hell did you let me finish? You should have pulled away."

"No. You should have pulled away like any other man who had some fucking respect for me would have done."

"But you liked it..."

"I liked it?" she said interrupting me. "You think I fucking liked it?"

"Yeah. That's what white girls do. Black girls front like they don't like it, but white girls will gladly swallow your cum."

"Well, this one won't," she yelled, scurrying around looking for her clothes.

Once I realized she was serious, I apologized over and over. But she wasn't beat.

"No, you meant to disrespect me, Mandingo, so why should I accept your apology?"

"Because I really am sorry."

"You're not sorry. If you were sorry, why did you laugh at me then?"

I'd almost forgotten that I had laughed. The whole situation was so fucking unexpected it caught me off guard. I didn't think she heard me. Still, I wasn't laughing at her. I was laughing at the situation. And she had to admit it, it was a funny-ass situation.

Who starts gagging like that after you take your dick out of their mouth?

At any rate, I didn't tell her what I was thinking. She probably wouldn't have looked at things the same way as I did.

Surprisingly, we were able to peace everything up that night. Or so I thought. To this day, Karen Steinberg stills mentions the time she says I disrespected her.

That night, though, after sulking for what seemed an eternity, she started complaining about not having an orgasm.

"How could you say that?" I asked. "You were screaming your fucking lungs out."

"I was screaming because I was in pain, you asshole, not because it felt good."

Karen Steinberg's words hit me like an unexpected sucker punch. But it wasn't because I was so big on her. I thought hard about what she said. Other women in my life had screamed like hell, too. I always thought that my dick was the bomb to them. But apparently I had the game totally fucked up.

"If I was hurting you, Karen, why didn't you say so?" I finally asked.

"Why should I?" she replied. "Your intention was to show me that black men have bigger dicks than white men and that you did. What reason did I have to just give up the fight before it even started?"

"All I know is that if someone is hurting you then you let them know. Hell, if it was a sister she would have said something," I said, trying more to convince myself than her.

"That's what you think, Mandingo, but you're wrong," she said sweetly. "Trust me, you're not just big because you're black. You're big for any man. And any woman who's had some of that big-ass dick was in pain. They were probably just too proud to tell you."

Out of nowhere Karen Steinberg started smiling.

"Correction. They probably didn't want to further inflate your already humongous ego."

"I'm not conceited."

"No one is saying you're conceited, but you do have a big-ass ego. Let a woman compliment you sometimes. You don't always have to give yourself props."

Clearly, my dick had Karen Steinberg talking crazy that night but her words did put a heart into what had previously just been some nice titties and a plump ass. Plus, I was still kinda upset about her not having an orgasm.

"Did I ever tell you that you're smart, Karen Steinberg?" I asked her.

"I guess I should be worried," she said. "You're complimenting me. What the hell do you want?"

"Why do I have to want something?" I asked.

"Because men always do," she said. "They treat you like shit on a regular basis because they want something. Then they act like you're the fucking queen of England."

"Well, regardless if I want something or not, I've honestly always thought you were smart. Why else would you be here?"

Karen Steinberg never answered me. She just rested her head on my shoulders.

"I'm still turned on," she had said. "My pussy is sore as all hell, but I'm still turned on. Do you think you can finish the job without trying to kill me?"

Without answering, I pulled her over to me and started kissing her neck. Before long, I started hungrily sucking on her titties.

It's baffling to me why I hadn't touched her titties before despite being so big on them. I guess she was right about me not caring about her. I'm not sure I ever started caring. But I was sure that I didn't like the fact that she didn't come. I remember thinking that the only way I was leaving that night without her having an orgasm was in a body bag.

After sucking on her titties long enough to get hard again, I laid on top of her and eased myself into her. She wrapped her legs around my back and we started grinding together in rhythm.

"Yes, Mandingo," she moaned. "This is how you're supposed to give a girl some of this big-ass dick."

I have to admit, it felt a lot better doing it slowly and carefully than it did acting like I was running a hundred yard dash.

She let me lead for a while then she asked me to let her get on top. I didn't care. As long as she didn't ask me to stop. I was possessed by the thought of making her come wildly and crazily.

Wildly and crazily, it's funny I use those words. That's exactly how Karen Steinberg started acting when she got on top.

When she got on top, she started grinding on me like she was riding a horse. It was kind of exotic. But it wasn't anything to write home bragging about. Then something changed. She started moaning really loud and hopping up and down harder and harder on my dick.

"Yes, Mandingo," she shouted. "Fuck me with this big black dick! Fuck the shit out of me you motherfucker!"

Karen Steinberg really started wilding out. She was bouncing on me like she was crazy. She had a hand full of my chest with her nails and was pounding me into the bed. It's a good thing I didn't have a girlfriend at the time or I would have been in trouble. I didn't care, though. The shit was starting to feel real good. And the way Karen Steinberg was acting was turning me the fuck on.

Before I had a chance to come the second time, Karen Steinberg let out a really loud shriek then slammed her pussy down hard on every inch of my dick. I could feel her pussy pulsating around my dick and before long she started to shake. Her eyes got really big and she became extremely quiet with the exception of her heart beating like an African drum roll.

She stayed that way for about three minutes then she lifted her head off of me and started kissing me on my neck and chest.

"Damn, this dick is good, Mandingo," she stammered. "Goddamn this dick is good."

Before I knew what was happening, her mouth had found its way back down to my dick. She was sucked it like I was about to give her a million dollars or something. Of course, it didn't take long for me to get ready to bust.

Since I felt it coming, this time I started pulling away. But she wouldn't let me pull away.

"No!" she yelled. "I want to taste you this time. I don't want to waste a single drop."

I never told Karen Steinberg what I'm about to say. In fact, I've never told any woman what I learned that night. I found out that if you don't just try to go for yourself and actually keep the woman's enjoyment in mind then you will enjoy the sex just as much as she does, if not more. And she may let you get away with a few things she would have ordinarily freaked out about.

I can't believe that she let me fuck her again after I came in her mouth. Then she let me come in her mouth again and swallowed it.

I have never been mad at Karen Steinberg since that day. Now, today, not only am I not mad at her but I love her. That's right—I love her. If you saw what I am seeing right now while Denise is undressing you would understand. I'm the luckiest man in the world right now because of a country-ass white girl named Karen Steinberg.

Like Don King says, "Only in America." Only in fucking America.

ABOUT THE AUTHOR

Sidibe Ibrahima, affectionately called "Sidi", was born and raised in Africa's Ivory Coast. In 1982 he moved to Germany and attended university. There, he developed his entrepreneurial spirit. In 1995, he returned to the Ivory Coast and opened Sidibe & Freres Distribution, an import/export company.

In 2000, able to speak seven different languages and write four, Sidi came to America. He got a job working at a jewelry store for $3.50 an hour and driving a taxicab. As soon as he managed to save $600, he opened his first bookstand in Harlem.

In addition to selling books, Sidi began reading them, many from new publishing companies, and sharing them with other book vendors. With his business savvy and his networking skills, Sidi expanded his business to five bookstands—one in every borough of New York City.

Over the years, Sidi has helped promote many authors—Teri Woods of Teri Woods Publishing, Shannon Holmes of Triple Crown, Danielle Santiago, author of A Little Ghetto Girl in Harlem, and Treasure Blue, author of Harlem Girl Lost to name but a few. On the distribution side, Sidi has assisted Culture Plus and A & B distributors and Say U Promise publication.

Recently, he's worked with Ashante Kahare, author of Homo Thug and has helped his novel to become a bestseller.

Sidi's "start small but think big" attitude has helped him become the most well-known seller of African American books in New York City. He is constantly sent books to review and blueline proofs to approve prior to going to press. Sidi has his finger on the pulse of the African American book patron and a natural instinct for and knowledge of the ever-increasing market for urban literature.

In response to market demand, Sidi has created Harlem Book Center (HBC), a publishing and distribution company based in Harlem. Its first release was *Fatou: An African Girl in Harlem*, a novel Sidi penned himself. Both HBC and "Fatou" are doing extremely well and Sidi expectations have already been surpassed. His hope is to grow HBC into a huge publishing and distribution conglomerate operating both nationally and internationally.

With his natural talents and instincts, Sidi has already accomplished many things in his young life. And his future promises to be exciting and successful. Be sure to visit Harlem Book Center at (www.harlembookcenter.com) or visit him online to keep abreast of current and ongoing projects.

Harlem Book Center
106West 137th Street Ste 5D
New York, NY 10030
Tel: +1 646/739-6429